MILLIONAIRE BOSS

A SECRET BABY ROMANCE

NATASHA L. BLACK

COPYRIGHT

The following story contains mature themes, strong language and sexual situations. It is intended for mature readers.

Cover Photographer: Wander Aguiar Photography
Model: Jaden Goetz

1

QUENTIN

There was nothing like a summer night. The North Carolina heat searing away the edges of the day and stinging on your skin the instant you walked out of the house faded and softened. As the sun seemed to melt and slip down the edge of the sky until it pooled on the horizon, it took the miserable humidity with it. In its place it left relief and a welcome breeze. It was like the temperature hovered so high it finally reached its capacity and cracked, and I felt like I could breathe.

Even better was a lazy summer night when I had nothing hanging over me, no expectations. When I just got a chance to relax and enjoy it. Those were rare. Life was busy and it felt like far too often my plans to just take in a night and savor it got steamrolled by something. I could spend the day absolutely determined to take a break and head out into my backyard for the evening, then get wrapped up in something and by the time I was able to pull away from it, I realized it was the middle of the night. Not that it stopped me from still wanting to head out. There were plenty of times when midnight found me tempted to wake up my fire pit and sit out there in the dark.

I stopped myself from doing it, willing myself into bed instead, but the longing was still there. But not that night. I finally had some time when I didn't have responsibilities and urgent needs pressing in around me, and I could actually have one of those coveted lazy summer nights. And I fully intended on absorbing every minute of it. Grabbing the tray of food I'd put together, I carried it outside onto my deck, then down the large staircase that led to my lawn. Despite not being able to spend much time in it, it was entirely possible my backyard was actually my favorite feature of my house. A lot of time, energy, and money went into creating the exact space I wanted, so when I did get the time to enjoy it, it was everything I could want.

That included the massive stone fire pit surrounded by large custom-created log benches and stools. They reminded me of the camping trips my family used to take when I was younger. My brothers and I would sit around the fire for as long as our parents let us, roasting anything we could figure out how to impale on the end of a stick or stuff into a sandwich maker. While we ate scorched hot dogs and stuck our fingers together with the remnants of s'mores, we told increasingly disturbing ghost stories with the singular goal of scaring the hell out of each other. There was the ongoing challenge to see which one would sneak up closer to the fire to get in more of the light, which would turn on their flashlight first, and which would try to make enough "accidental" noise to lure our parents out of the tent to stop the story.

This pit was a bit more sophisticated than the ring we built from whatever rocks we could find scattered around in the woods, and I rarely had to worry about critters scurrying out of the logs when they lit. Our snacks had gotten less messy and were usually accompanied by beer. We hadn't told ghost stories in years. But the spirit and sentiment were still there.

My brothers and parents were already sitting around the blazing bonfire. My father occasionally prodded the logs, sending cascades of sparks up into the darkening sky.

"Here we go," I said. "A few more things to dig into."

My youngest brother stared at the tray as I set it down.

"Seriously? We're going to make snakes?" he asked. "Are you sure you're the oldest brother?"

"I hate when you call them that," my mother said, shuddering. "I never hear the whole sentence, and it always gives me the heebie-jeebies."

My brother Nick lifted up from the seat beside Darren and grabbed one of the pieces of dough stretched out on a plate in the middle of the tray.

"What are you talking about, Darren? These things are delicious," he said.

They were nothing more than canned biscuit dough wrapped around the end of a stick and roasted over the fire until done, then rolled in butter, but they were always a favorite treat on those long-ago camping trips. Cheap and fast, they were an easy way for my parents to feed their brood of four boys, and because they could be dipped in either cinnamon sugar or salt once buttered, they pleased everybody. As we got a little older, we'd graduated to adding garlic or sometimes chili powder to the savory ones, but the cinnamon sugar option was left untouched, a sacred part of summer.

Unless you were Darren and thought you were too grown-up in all of your twenty-three years to wrap a piece of biscuit dough around a stick and shove it in a fire. Too bad for him. I'd eat a can of biscuits' worth myself. I grabbed my own piece of dough and got it toasting, taking a draw of my beer as I did. All in all, I was feeling pretty good about life in general. My racing company was doing well. My bank account was nicely full and getting more so every day. I had my house, my brothers, my parents, my friends.

"Are you seeing anyone special?" my mother asked.

Shit.

And then there was that.

I took another long sip of my beer and looked at the bottle to determine if there was enough left in it to get me through the rest of the conversation or if I'd need another.

"No," I answered after determining I could carry through.

"Are you seeing anyone at all?" she asked.

"No. I've been really busy. Not exactly a lot of time to devote to dating," I said.

"That's a shame. You really need to meet someone, Quentin. A nice woman who will understand your career and appreciate your lifestyle. Someone to come home to at night and take care of you."

And I was officially wrong about the beer. Getting up, I downed the last of the bottle in my hand and headed over to the cooler to select another. A quick snap with the opener mounted on the table removed the cap, and I headed back to my bench.

"Not interested right now, Mom," I said.

"But why?" she asked, her eyes wide as if she couldn't possibly grasp what I was telling her.

It gave me a flicker of guilt. Just a flicker. Not enough to change my stance.

"You know what happened with Victoria," I said.

My brothers groaned, remembering my disastrous last relationship far too well.

"She wasn't right for you," Mom relented. "But there has to be someone out there who won't be like her."

"And maybe one day I'll find her," I said. "For now, I'm good with living the single life."

The truth was, I hadn't had very much luck with women. It seemed the ones I encountered were far more interested in my money than they were in me as a person. Anyone could have been attached to the other end of the bank card as long as the women got to be the ones to swipe it. I'd been burned more than once, and I'd officially gotten it out of my system. That type of relationship had no appeal to me, and I'd much rather just focus on the single life.

Not that it was really settling. My life was far from boring and even further from empty. Full of family and work, it kept me running most of the time. And I was fine with that.

Mom was merciful in letting the conversation drop before I made much more of a dent in the beer cooler. The same couldn't be said for Darren. For all his scoffing over the biscuit dough, he roasted at least six of them and stuffed himself with hot dogs and s'mores on top of it. With nearly every bite he took a swig or two of beer, and by the time my parents were ready to leave for the night, he was feeling no pain. The four of us brothers hung out around the fire for another hour, giving the alcohol enough time to soak into every fiber of his being, join up with more that he downed during that hour, and render him a mess.

"Let me get the guest room ready for him," I told Vince and Nick as we watched Darren dance around the fire to one of his favorite songs. "No need for him to try to leave tonight."

"Well, at least you can say you throw a good party," Nick said.

"Yeah," I said with a laugh as I headed up the stairs back onto the deck. "Nothing says party hard like your mother grilling you about why you don't have a nice wife and a gaggle of babies."

"I don't think she mentioned a gaggle of babies," Vince pointed out.

"Not in words," I said, turning around to face them and using two fingers to swirl melodramatic circles in front of my eyes. "I saw it in her eyes."

I left my laughing brothers and went to the guest room to make sure it had everything Darren would need to crash there that night. After adding a bottle of water to the nightstand, I went back down to help Nick get him upstairs. We yanked off his shoes and jeans, rolled him into the bed, and covered him up. I couldn't resist snapping a picture of my drunk baby brother drooling on the pillow before turning off the light and heading out of the room. That would make a fun addition to the family group chat the next day.

After saying goodbye to my other two brothers, I locked up the house and went for a shower. I stood under the hot water for a long time after the smoky smell of the fire washed away from my skin and hair just to let my muscles relax. When I was done, I threw on a pair of boxers and slid into bed. My eyes flickered over to the tablet on my nightstand. The screen was dark, but I could almost hear all the emails and messages inside waiting for me to reply.

It was late, but not so late that I couldn't get some work in. I thought about getting just a little bit done, spending at least part of the night being productive. Even when I wasn't at the office or the racetrack on any given day, the work didn't stop. There was far more to be done for the company than just the races themselves, and the messages, questions, and requests never stopped. I started to reach for the tablet, then stopped myself.

I wasn't going to do it. I'd gotten a rare, treasured night completely off, and I wasn't going to ruin it by burying myself back in work again. I had the next week free, and then it was back to racing season. Once that started, it was going to be all stress and schedules so busy they were bursting at the seams until the season came to an end. The whole point of taking the time off before the season got underway was to relax, and that was exactly what I was going to do. For the next week, it was all about giving myself the time to chill, rejuvenate myself, and prepare for the inevitable, unavoidable chaos to come.

Rather than picking up the tablet, I called out to my virtual assistant to turn on some music to help me sleep, turned off the lights, and closed my eyes with a long exhale.

2

MERRY

"Shit, shit, shit, I'm gonna be late!"

My clothes were scattered all over the floor, a bra was hanging from the back of a chair in the corner, and I couldn't find one of my shoes.

It was nowhere near as exciting as it sounded. It wasn't the fun of a carefree night. Or even an ill-advised, but still thrilling, night. It was the sheer chaos on the morning of the interview for a job I would kill for. I wasn't usually one for hyperbole and definitely wouldn't want to just start wishing violence on everybody around me, but for this job, I might make an exception. Working for the Freeman Racing could slingshot my career to a whole new level.

Being a social media consultant gave me the opportunity to work with a lot of interesting people, but the unfortunate thing about it was the smaller clients often thought they could pick up the skills themselves and start doing it on their own rather than relying on me—*thought* being the operative word. More often than not, they'd depend on me to build up their social media presence for a few months, see the benefits, then decide they could do it themselves and let me go. Inevitably a good portion of them would realize the whole reason they'd hired me in the first place was because they didn't know how to run their platform effectively.

That meant I got repeat business, but it was frustrating as hell. I hated seeing the mess they created out of what I built and having to fix it. It was especially aggravating when I realized it was my name attached to what they made out of it. Of course, there were other times when the smaller companies and private clients actually did pick up on the skills and were able to keep it going on their own. That was a victory of its own kind for me. In the end, the point of my job was to help companies gain more visibility and success through the effective use of social media.

But it all boiled down to the same thing. I was a professional transient. Not the wander the streets and sleep under the bridge type, but the bounce from post to post, gig to gig, always looking for work even when I had it type. That didn't sit well with me. It was exciting when I first started. In those first few months when I got my business going, I felt like a powerful contemporary woman standing on my own two feet and running my empire. At least, the beginning of an empire.

The novelty wore off after a while, and I started longing for something more stable. I set my sights on just that, a big company that would need their social media built but then sustained. Larger companies didn't have the time to keep up with that sort of daily activity, meaning if I could land the position with Freeman Racing, I might be able to settle in for the long haul. That sounded glorious.

All I needed to do was impress the woman doing the interview, then prove myself as indispensable. No pressure.

"Ugh, I have nothing in this damn closet!" I complained aloud, tossing pieces aside like a crazed lunatic.

I put on the outfit I finally settled on, a dark blue suit with a pencil skirt and blazer that nipped in at my waist and added my favorite heels. Topping off the look with a strand of my grandmother's pearls, I looked in the hall mirror to fluff my hair one last time and rushed out to my pale blue Mini Cooper gleaming in the driveway. Before cranking the ignition, I checked the directions to the complex one more time. My GPS could guide me, but I never liked to rely fully on technology. Ironic as that was considering my career path, I was never one to put my belief solely on the little lines on the screen and the monotonous, perpetually pissed-off-sounding woman telling me what turns to take. Just in case she wasn't made fully aware of obstacles that might show up in my path, or the satellites decided to go on strike while I was midtrip, I wanted to still have some grasp of where I was.

That's where my printed directions and maps came in. A quick glance over them gave me a heads-up for the journey, and I headed on my way. The day was beautiful, with the weather being not too hot yet. I was tempted to roll the windows down so I could enjoy the feeling of the summer air on my face as I zoomed around the backroads of the lush North Carolina greenery. But I had to remember my hair and that I didn't want to show up at the interview looking a mess. I'd reward myself with the rolling the windows down on the way home if the interview went well, I promised myself.

Not wanting to even begin to risk being late, I'd left half an hour earlier than I really needed to. But I was glad for it when I ended up twisted around and showed up at the complex only fifteen minutes early.

A man in a small guardhouse at the gate directed me to the right parking lot and handed me access credentials. Finding the lot, I parked and stepped out of the car, taking a moment to smooth my skirt and take a few breaths to calm myself. I was excited about the possibilities that lay ahead and felt good about my chances. I was skilled at what I did and had done plenty of research into the company's current social media presence. I was more than armed with a thorough and, if I did say so myself, an effective plan to demonstrate the potential for the platforms. But wanting it didn't guarantee I'd land the position, so the nerves still created butterflies in my stomach.

When I felt ready, I grabbed my bag and headed in search of the location of my appointment. Minette "call me Minnie" Freeman was sweet and welcoming over the phone when I spoke to her, so I was looking forward to meeting her. I found the right office building and signed in at the front desk, offering a smile to the woman sitting there. She directed me to the waiting area, and I drew in another breath before taking a seat, wanting to look as calm and put together as I could when she arrived.

When she did, it was amidst a cloud of Chanel and in a summer dress with flip-flops. I suddenly felt extremely overdressed. Apparently, this wasn't a business attire type of office. But I'd rather look too formal and professional than not professional enough, so I fell into step behind her with confidence. As we walked toward her office, I listened to Minnie go on and on about her family and the company. I already knew it was her oldest son, Quentin, who owned and ran the business, but she was the one who handled most of the hiring. He wasn't exactly a people person.

Which was the ideal segue into her letting out a deep sigh as she dropped into the chair behind her desk and declared she knew Quentin, and the company, definitely needed my help.

"There is almost no social media presence on any of the platforms," she confided. "And in 2020, that's unheard of. I suppose I don't really need to tell you that."

I smiled politely and shook my head.

"No, you're right. Social media is vital to business success in today's marketplace. Consumers are more tech-savvy than ever and tend to glean most of their opinions about a business based on what they can find using an internet search. This means they are most likely to make decisions for their spending and brand loyalty based on the internet, most importantly social media. This is how they determine if a business fits with their personal interests and needs, if they feel they can relate to them and trust them, and also where they find information about them. It's hard to gain interest or build up an audience when there is no way for them to know what you're offering. That's where social media comes in. And I'll be honest. I did do some preliminary exploring of the current presence," I said.

"And it wasn't good," Minnie concluded flatly.

I couldn't help but laugh. This was a woman I could definitely see enjoying working with.

"Since you put it that way, no, it wasn't," I said with a smile. "But it could be. The good part about having next to no social media presence is that you have a fairly blank canvas to work with. Rather than having to try to undo mistakes and rebuild a reputation that has been damaged by bad social media, you can just build from the bottom up and create an impressive presence. That's where I come in." I reached down for my messenger bag and took out the plan

I'd drafted. "I took the liberty of putting together a plan for the first few weeks and months of a new social media campaign for Freeman Racing. You can glance over it and see one direction we could go. Of course, this is only one approach, and there are many different options."

Minnie took the file folder from me and opened it, spreading the papers out on the desk in front of her. It felt oddly exposing to have my work spread out like that in front of me. I knew what every word said and felt completely confident in what I put together, but somehow it made me feel vulnerable to watch her look over it like that. She nodded a few times, making sounds that could either be acknowledgement or her simply noting places she would want to make changes.

It took only a few minutes before she looked up at me and smiled.

"I have to say, I'm impressed. Your reputation is fantastic, of course, but I know you haven't worked for any companies on quite the scale as this one. It would be a much larger project," she said.

"Absolutely," I admitted. "It would be far more extensive than anything I've ever had. But the scope of it means I would be able to focus completely on this campaign. You would have my absolute undivided attention, and I would create something customized exclusively for the flexible and changing needs of the company. Utilizing my skills means others in the company don't have to try to keep up and can focus on the other elements of their jobs. My professional experience also means I would be able to broaden the targeted demographics and create more involvement among fans."

Minnie nodded and I knew the job was mine. It took everything in me to not jump up and explode with excitement. She reached into a drawer in her desk and pulled out a contract that she slid across the desk to me.

"This is the initial contract," she said. "If you would look over it and let me know if you have any questions or things you'd like to discuss."

I wanted to just sign my name on the dotted line as fast as I possibly could, but that's never good business practice. Instead, I forced myself to slow down and scan through the contract, reviewing all the terms and expectations. I was pleasantly surprised to see I didn't even need to attempt to negotiate for better pay. The offer included in the contract was already exceptionally generous and far more than I would have made with any other client.

When I was finished, I smiled at her.

"Do you have a pen I could use?" I asked politely.

Minnie grinned at me and offered me a gold engraved pen that was filled with vibrant purple ink. I would expect nothing less of her. She watched me sign my name, then stood, extending her hand to me.

"Congratulations and welcome aboard. I look forward to working with you," she said.

I let out a long breath, feeling my shoulders relax as I smiled.

"Thank you. I do, too," I told her.

"You come on back on Monday. Quentin is taking his first vacation in a long while this week, but he'll be back then," she said.

"His first vacation?" I asked, tilting my head to the side with curiosity.

"Yes. That man refuses to take a break. He does nothing but work. Doesn't even take the time to breathe half the time, I think. But his brothers, father, and I finally convinced him to take this week off so he could be rested up and have a good head on his shoulders when the race season starts up again," she said.

"Oh," I said, my smile slipping as I nodded, processing what she'd just told me about her son.

"Don't worry," Minnie said as if she could sense my nervousness to meet the man who would be my direct boss. "He might be an old curmudgeon before he earned the old, but he can be a softy, too. You'll see. He'll like you."

We chatted for a few more minutes before I disengaged from the conversation and headed home to decompress. Just as I promised myself, I rolled down the windows and enjoyed the flow of the wind through my hair as I drove. Just before getting home, I stopped for a celebratory bottle of wine and looked forward to a barefoot evening on the patio and a bubble bath.

3

QUENTIN

I still wasn't completely convinced about the idea of taking regular vacations. It seemed like everywhere I looked, people were living the opposite schedule of life I would think was normal. Every other day they posted pictures of their most recent getaway, making it seem like most of their life was a vacation and they occasionally returned for a week or two of normalcy. Of course, I was on the extreme end of the spectrum in the opposite direction, according to my parents and brothers. I hadn't taken a vacation since those camping trips of my youth. I just didn't have the time for it. The trips dwindled down by the time I was in the later years of high school, and then when I was in college out of state, I didn't make the trip back to join the few that popped up while Darren was growing up.

Life after college got far too crammed to fit in long stretches of doing nothing purely for the sake of doing nothing. I was too committed to putting as much work and effort into reaching my goals to purposely have long days of making no progress. It seemed to me if I wasn't doing something it needed to be because of serious illness or grievous bodily harm. Considering the industry that I dedicated my life to, there was always the possibility of the latter, and the former was just something all humans needed to be prepared for in life. I would much rather keep grinding on the days when I could so if the need popped up to spend time out of commission, I didn't feel like I was getting too far behind.

That's why it wasn't the easiest thing in the world for my family to finally convince me to take a vacation this past week. All of them were worried about the amount of stress I constantly put on myself and insisted I needed to take some time so my brain didn't melt, or my heart didn't stop, or any number of other needlessly graphic and overdramatic warnings they came up with each time they sat me down. I didn't want to take the time off. Of course I was tired and had worked myself to the bone, but there was always more to do. Always more I *could* do. More success to be made. It felt strange to just say I would willingly not do any of it. It finally took my mother looking legitimately worried and my brother's promising they would make a bunch of extra work for me when I did go back so I felt productive that they convinced me to take the vacation.

I'll admit it was kind of nice to not have to wake up before the sun. Not that I stayed in bed for terribly much longer than that on any given morning. It was hard-wired into me to start the day too early and end it too late. But there was a certain amount of luxury in opening my eyes and knowing I didn't actually have to get out of bed at that exact moment. I could stretch out and just lie there. I could roll over and watch TV for as long as I felt like, stuffing snacks in my mouth and drinking too much soda.

There was also an appeal to being able to roam around the house in my boxers, float around in the pool, and actually use the backyard I so often stared at longingly through the window when I was in my home office working. But there was also the pressing feeling I was missing something. I kept wondering what was going on at the office or what everyone was doing. I called up there so many times Glenda, the receptionist, redirected my number to my mother, who promptly blocked it.

That didn't seem like the best way to treat the head of the company, but, as she crisply informed me when I circumvented her block by using my landline, mother trumps CEO. At least in most situations.

So, I relented and did my prescribed time. But it was finally my first day back at the Freeman Racing complex... and there was a woman in my office I had never seen before.

I stood several feet away from the chair where she was sitting, staring at her and flipping through the Rolodex of my mind to try to identify her. Maybe she was someone I'd met at one of the many events I went to each season. Could she be the daughter of one of the drivers? Of one of my competitors? Of a vendor? Could she be the vendor herself? A reporter? None of the options rolling through my mind made anything click. When I'd first arrived at the complex that morning, the guard didn't say anything about a new employee, so that wasn't any help.

What also wasn't any help was I couldn't get my eyes off her. She wasn't just unfamiliar, she was gorgeous. Dark hair hung like mahogany in a loose knot at the back of her neck, her skin was smooth and creamy, and when she stood up, her sundress clung to lush, unapologetic curves. When she glanced up and noticed I was standing there, huge almond eyes and a bright smile completed the package of essentially my ideal woman. Never in my career had I had any difficulty keeping things professional, but this woman might just be enough to attempt me.

She took a step toward me and reached out her hand.

"Hi," she said. "You must be Mr. Freeman. I'm Merry. I'm here to make you social."

I shook her hand, but I wasn't entirely sure what she was talking about. Social? My mind was starting to traipse down the ridiculous path of wondering if one of my parents had hired an actress from a local community theater to pretend to be my girlfriend and desensitize me to the concept when I remembered. Mom had talked about hiring a social media consultant to get me on my game. Nodding, I released her hand and walked around to sit across from her.

"Right. The social media consultant," I said.

"Yes," she answered, settling back into the chair. "It's a pleasure to finally get to meet you, Mr. Freeman."

She was probably ten years younger than me, which made me sound even older when she called me "Mr. Freeman." I'd been lying if I said it didn't turn me on at least a little, but I needed to bring it back down to the usual level of my office.

"Call me Quentin," I instructed. "What do you need from me, Merry?"

I folded my hands on the desk in front of me and stared at her, waiting for her to explain why I got to work that morning to find her already waiting in my office. People getting a jump on me when it came to starting my day wasn't something I was a big fan of in any circumstances, but when that person was a young, sexy woman who I could see proving a distraction, I was particularly not a fan.

"As you probably already know, your mother hired me last week. I got here early this morning so I could hit the ground running. She showed me my office and has given me access to the accounts so I can start working on them. I don't know how much she told you about our interview and the plans I've already laid out..."

"None," I said, cutting her off. "I was on vacation last week, and she hasn't told me anything about you other than that she was looking into hiring a social media consultant."

A stung expression flickered briefly over Merry's eyes, but she quickly rebounded.

"No problem. I brought along the plans I put together if you want to look over them," she said.

I nodded and she pulled a file out of a messenger bag at her feet. Glancing over the pages, I listened as she rattled off essentially what I was reading. She threw around terms like 'scheduled posting' and 'click-through,' while making the fans of my company sound like a bunch of tokens she was trying to collect. I would be the first to admit social media was not my thing, and I probably didn't understand everything she was trying to get across to me just because it wasn't something I much cared about. So, I let her talk right until she mentioned going around the complex taking pictures.

Merry stopped short when she saw me hold up my hand and shake my head.

"No," I told her.

"Excuse me?" she asked.

"No," I repeated. "I'm not going to grant you free access to the complex so you can go around taking pictures for who knows what use."

She gave me a slightly condescending look.

"The use is to post on your various platforms to give followers a glimpse into the company. You want to seem like more than just a facade. Letting them see more behind the scenes, people who work here, the pond, the test tracks... it makes them feel more like they are a part of something rather than just drooling fans," she told me. "The more invested they feel, the more money they'll spend."

Her tongue ran briefly over her nude-painted lips, and I had to force myself not to stare at them, to keep my attention on the conversation at hand.

"You need to understand there is proprietary information you can't share. There are things throughout this complex that aren't just openly offered up for the public, and can't be shared with my competitors," I told her.

Merry shifted in her seat, and the look on her face melted into a smile that said she thought I was an idiot.

"Yes, I understand that," she said, her voice noticeably slowing. "I do know how to do my job." She stood up. "Thank you for meeting with me this morning."

"Well, you didn't give me much of a choice," I said, standing and giving her a tight smile.

She gathered the papers on my desk and shoved them back into her messenger bag, tossing it over her shoulder.

"There are some other people Minnie mentioned she would like me to meet, and then I need to get started. Your presence needs a tremendous amount of work and improvement. I've got my work cut out for me," she said.

I watched her leave, noting the sway of her hips as she walked, and wondered how in fresh hell this was going to work. Merry didn't choose her words lightly, and the way she threw my mother's name out there was like drawing a line in the sand. She wanted to make sure I knew she was already familiar with my mother and they were on the same team, like she had gotten Mom's approval, so she wasn't as concerned with what I thought of her. So not only was she beautiful, confident, and sexy, making it hard enough to think about working around her, but she talked to me like I was disconnected from the world and had an attitude about it. This was going to be delightful.

I needed to have a few words with my mother. Not even bothering to turn my computer on, I left my office to find Mom. My first stop was her office, and I half expected to find Merry already there. But I didn't. In fact, I didn't find either of them. Her office was dark, the door closed. Next, I tried the breakroom, but it, too, was empty. Mysteriously, she was missing from every place I searched for her, and I wondered if she had already gotten wind I was on my way and planned on ducking me for the day.

4

MERRY

I had to commend myself for my mature and professional behavior. I managed to get all the way through that infuriating and condescending conversation with Quentin Freeman without so much as pointing out the various ways he was proving himself to be an arrogant, insufferable jackass, or telling him exactly what bridge he could jump off. It seemed like a victory to me. As it was, I walked away from the office with my hands clenched into fists so tightly my fingernails cut into my palms and made me wish I hadn't bothered to go into the salon the week before the interview to top off my professional look with a set of acrylics. It wasn't like I needed them for the position, anyway.

I made it all the way out of the building and into the fresh air of the morning before letting out an exasperated sound that was just a little bit too close to a growl. My grandmother went to a lot of effort when I was young to teach me how to be a lady. While the idea of growling at people in public wasn't specifically mentioned, I was fairly certain it was an unspoken no-no. Especially in a work setting. And especially at my boss.

My boss. Just thinking those words filled me with aggravation all over again. Of everybody who could have been the successful and wealthy CEO of the company I was now working for, it had to be the infuriating and gorgeous man who struck me silent the instant I saw him. If the social media of this place was halfway fucking decent maybe I'd have gotten a better grasp of who everybody was around here and not to be so shocked when he came into the office.

That would have made my position obsolete and I wouldn't be in this situation, but that was beside the point. At least I wouldn't have come up with a vision in my mind of what the head of a racing company looked like, then gotten knocked for a loop when *he* walked into the office. Quentin was hot. Stupidly hot. He was tall, dark, and brooding, and even with clothes on it looked like he was crafted out of marble. But he was also disconnected, stuffy, and full of himself.

Granted, he was also an eligible millionaire many a woman had drooled over but not landed. When I heard there was an opening at Freeman Racing for the exact type of position I was champing at the bit to get, I asked around about the company and did a little research. All the pictures I could find related to the company had groups of people in them. There were never any specific images of one person or another, making it almost impossible for me to get familiar with the Freeman family or who was who without doing some deep-dive searching I simply didn't have time to do. That meant when I stumbled on the stories and blogs about women trying to land Quentin and getting quickly rebuffed, I didn't have an image of who they were talking about.

Now I most certainly did. Not only did I know how sexy

he was, but also how cold and unpleasant he could be. That was not a combination I was interested in having anything to do with. Who wanted a man who didn't give a person a chance to prove themselves before he went all caveman on them? Definitely not me. I didn't want to believe the rumors that most of the women flinging themselves at his feet were only doing it to sink their claws into his millions and set themselves up for trophy wife glory throughout at least the next few years, then settle into alimony and the reality show circuit. But now that I'd had a chance to talk to Quentin, I could absolutely see why that would be the only reason any woman would put that much effort into trying to land him.

As long as he didn't talk, he could be nice to be in a room with.

I closed my eyes and shook my head, filling my lungs with a deep breath to try to calm myself down. I had to do my best not to let him get to me on my first day. This was not how I wanted to spend the first four hours of my time working at what amounted to my dream job. Before that run-in, I was so excited, and I was determined to keep feeling excited. I wasn't going to let him take that away from me. Constant contact with him wasn't necessary for me to do my job. I was more than capable of whipping their social media into shape and helping them storm into visibility with only the bare minimum of interactions with Quentin. And that's exactly what I intended to do.

Minnie was waiting for me across the complex in the coffee room of a smaller building. She was leaned against the counter, staring out a window as she stirred something in a mug that smelled like strong peppermint tea.

"Hi," I said as I walked in and headed directly for the coffee maker.

"Well, by the look on your face I can only guess you already met Quentin," she said.

I slammed the top of the single-cup maker down onto the pod a bit too hard and shoved a mug into place as I nodded.

"Yes, I did." I glanced over at her and sighed. "I'm sorry. I shouldn't be acting like this."

"Don't apologize. From personal experience, you probably *should* be acting like this. There's a reason that man doesn't have a personal assistant. Or a secretary. He is my firstborn, and I love him with all my heart, but he has a stubborn streak in him, and I don't know if he ever learned how to play nicely with others. At least not consistently. He can be a good guy. Really. So, what did he do?" she asked.

I took a long sip of coffee and shook my head, plastering on a smile.

"You know what? Nothing. I'm just overreacting," I said.

"Somehow I doubt that. You don't have to pretend," Minnie said.

"No. Seriously. I just got myself worked up because I wanted to impress him so much, and I let it get to me. Now, you said you wanted me to meet some people," I said.

"Absolutely. Let's go."

She spent the rest of the morning and early afternoon showing me around the complex and introducing me to the team working there. I knew the complex was expansive and far more complicated than just the family, but I was surprised by just how many people there were working behind the scenes. It was perfect for putting together galleries of pictures and posting content about the team and what went on at the complex when there wasn't a race happening.

Of course, as soon as I thought about that, my thoughts went right back to being in the office with Quentin that morning and getting chided for suggesting taking pictures. It was as if he was expecting me to throw open the personnel files and scan them into Twitter. Just thinking about it got me worked up again, and I had to talk myself down. Focusing on taking pictures of the building and the staff at work helped to bring my focus back to what I was doing. After lunch, Minnie had work she needed to do, so she set me loose on the complex by myself.

As much as I liked her and enjoying spending time with her, it was nice just being left with my own mind and being able to go where I wanted to go and get a feel of the place on my own. Hopefully I would be working there for a good while, and I wanted to be able to get myself around comfortably. It also let me snap pictures and take notes without feeling like I needed to explain each one to Minnie. I was sipping a cool drink to ward off the intensity of the heat when I looped back around to the test track deep in the complex. Minnie had already given me a quick glimpse of the track and of the bikes lined up, gleaming at the front of the building, but I wanted to do a bit more exploring.

I stepped into the shade for a brief moment just to get relief from the blazing sunlight and realized there was someone at the track. At first, I felt embarrassed to be there, like I'd gotten caught and needed to scurry away. Then I remembered the personalized credentials now around my neck and Minnie's invitation to explore to my heart's content. I hadn't snuck onto the grounds and wasn't doing anything clandestine. Quentin's words must have gotten to me more than I thought, and that aggravated me.

The man at the track wasn't there when Minnie and I were there earlier, but the longer I looked at him, the more familiar he seemed. I knew I'd seen his face before. As I walked up to the track, he glanced up from the bike he was working on and smiled.

"Hi," he said. "Can I help you?"

His smile was genuine and bright, his offer of help sincere and not a way of asking what the hell I was doing there.

"No," I said, smiling and shaking my head. "I'm just looking around. I'm Merry."

"Oh, the new social media consultant," he said.

I looked at him strangely, and he laughed.

"My mom told me she'd hired you and that today was your first day. I think you came by to meet me earlier, but I had to go to the parts shop." He wiped his hands on the cloth hanging from his belt. "I'm Darren Freeman."

Recognition hit me, and I nodded, reaching out to shake his hand.

"Right. The youngest of the brothers," I said. "And the racer of the family."

"That's right," he said. "Are you settling in all right? I know it's just your first day, but are you feeling okay about everything?"

It took me aback. This man was sweet and quiet. Absolutely nothing like his oldest brother. I also couldn't help but realize I didn't feel at all drawn to him. That was frustrating as hell to realize. I wanted to think there was just something about being on the complex surrounded by the wealth and adrenaline that was getting me going in Quentin's office. It wasn't him. Not the arrogant, pigheaded caveman.

And yet here I was, facing a younger, perhaps slightly

softer version of him, and I felt nothing. He was a sweet guy who I could have fun talking to, but that was it. I sighed. That was just as well. I was already feeling a twinge of guilt for the thoughts that went through my head when I saw Quentin. There was no need to add another layer of unprofessionalism to it.

"I'm doing fine so far," I told Darren. "But you could help me with something. I'll admit, I don't know the first thing about racing. That's kind of embarrassing to tell you considering I'm working here now. I've done some research and watched a lot of videos, but I don't think that really gives me a full vision of what it's like and what it means to your family. Do you think you could tell me about it? Give me an overview of what racing means to you and what the season's like? Tell me what goes on at the complex throughout the year and what races are like? It'll help me to have a fuller idea of the company and what it does so I can create the most effective campaign."

He nodded like he wasn't quite sure of the ramble of words that just came out at him, but he happily started talking. I stayed there with him for the rest of the afternoon, learning about the company and about racing in general, and the youngest of the Freeman boys proved very helpful. That night when I got to my car, I turned around and glared at the building where I'd met with Quentin. I swore I could, and would, do this, no matter what he thought of me. Or what I thought of him, to be honest. I would just have to compartmentalize. He was hot and frustrating, but that didn't matter. It couldn't matter. Him thinking I was an idiot, on the other hand, needed to change. But that was no problem. I could absolutely prove him wrong on that.

5

QUENTIN

I walked slowly around the bike, taking in all the details and surveying the changes Darren had made. He'd been working on the new race bike for several weeks, and it was exciting to finally be able to see the finished product. It wasn't an uncommon mistake for people who weren't familiar with the racing industry to assume I was the one who did the actual racing. After all, I owned the company and was the one in control of the team. But that wasn't my role in the empire I'd built. I was the one responsible for the business element, for managing strategy and powering Darren to victory. He was a skilled and successful racer already, and his eyes were always focused firmly ahead. There were many more accomplishments on the horizon, and he wanted to be the best of the best. Just being good enough or even raking in wins throughout the season wasn't enough for him. If he wasn't winning every race or wasn't winning by enough of a margin, he didn't feel like he did well enough.

Not that he was a bad loser or was too arrogant to believe someone could be better than him. Quite the opposite, actually. Darren was humble and determined. The quietest and most in his head of the four of us. It wasn't that he thought he had to be the absolute best because no one could be better than him. It wasn't the competition that got to him, the other racers or the other teams. Instead, he was always in competition with himself and wanting to push harder to new levels of success and achievement. He wanted to do better simply because he believed he *could* do better. He would be the first to tell you he got a rush out of a good race and enjoyed when his competitors did well. He wouldn't want to be a winner because all the other racers failed miserably. There was no fun, no sense of pride or honor in being at the top when everyone else was in a heap beneath him.

Darren was determined if he was going to be the best, it was going to be because he earned it. I had absolutely no doubt he would earn it. And once he did, he would have his chance to get a bit of a big head and enjoy the prestige. But for now, it was all about figuring out ways he could do better, starting with crafting the fastest and most efficient bike possible for the upcoming races. We were going over the new specs on his bike and discussing possibilities for other modifications when out of the corner of my eye I saw someone stalking toward the test track.

At first, I thought it might be Glenda, the receptionist. As many times as I tried to tell her it wasn't my fault, she still got frustrated at me when women called the desk. Unfortunately, it wasn't an odd occurrence for one or more women to call the complex incessantly, insisting on talking with me. Several just assumed they would be able to charm their way past the receptionist, not realizing she'd been working with my family for years and could give seriously zero fucks who we were or how powerful people thought we were because of what I'd built.

The truth was Glenda saw past everything and knew every one of the members of the family exceptionally well. She'd worked for my father's business before Darren was even born, which meant the four of us boys were still just kids to her. She wasn't impressed by us and wasn't going to be convinced she should be. And she most certainly wasn't impressed by the women who liked to throw around their names or try to convince her they had some sort of intimate knowledge of me. I couldn't count how many times she'd told me of the women who called, trying to get through with a story about having met me at one event or another, and that I had given her my phone number with the insistence they call me.

Of course, they would have no way of knowing I would never give the information for the front desk of the office building if I wanted to talk to somebody directly. Instead, they would get my personal cell number, or at the very least the number to the phone in my office. She was quick to shut them down and never filtered any of them through to me, for which I was grateful. But that didn't stop her from scolding me about them wasting her time and tangling up her phone lines. But that day it wasn't Glenda. Instead, Mom was stomping toward me and she looked pissed.

Darren snickered and walked away, leaving me to be cornered by our mother. Whatever was wrong, I was alone to deal with her wrath. She wasn't even all the way to me when one finger jutted out from her hand directed right at my face and the other hand planted firmly on her hip. I knew that posture. That was the angry mother ready to scold posture. I'd seen it when my brothers and I tracked mud through the house when we were little. I'd seen it again when we were teenagers and stayed out past our curfew doing the stupid things teenage boys did when they stayed out past their curfew. And I was seeing it now.

Only this time, I didn't know what had gotten her riled up, so I didn't have the opportunity to prepare my defense.

"My boy, we're going to have a talk about how you treat new employees," she announced when she got to me.

Her arms crossing over her chest made me shrink back slightly. It felt ridiculous for a grown-ass man to react like that, this was my mama and I loved her, but she could be tough as nails. And now I knew exactly what she was talking about.

"I didn't mean to upset her," I said.

There was really no point in trying to play dumb or waiting for Mom to tell me what she was angry about. The only new employee we'd had recently was Merry, and there was no questioning if I'd made her upset the day before when she surprised me in my office.

"But you didn't mean to welcome her or make her feel like she's a part of the team, either, did you?" Mom asked.

"She's not really part of the team," I pointed out. "She's only worked here for what, thirty-six hours? I don't think that really constitutes her being considered one of us."

"I don't care how long she's worked here. She's an employee, and as the owner of the company, and just a human being I raised to be a decent person, you should have treated her with more respect. I raised my sons to be good men, and that means being polite and respectful, even if you don't particularly like the person. Which, by the way, I wouldn't understand because I think she's delightful."

I stood there taking the tongue-lashing, knowing it bothered Mom when one of her sons didn't live up to her vision for what a good man was supposed to be. Not that I always agreed with it, and definitely didn't always live up to it. I wasn't the kind to gush and fawn over a woman just because she was there. Especially when it came to my business. I didn't think I was in any way rude or intolerable toward Merry. I didn't gather up in a hug and invite her to Thanksgiving dinner, but I also didn't yell at her and tell her I didn't want her strolling into my office whenever she wanted to.

I also didn't share with her any of the less than professional thoughts she made course through my head. That was the most difficult part of it.

"Maybe I wasn't the most welcoming of new bosses," I relented, "but even you have to admit it's a bit annoying she went and pouted to my mother. That's not exactly professional."

"She didn't come pouting to me," Mom corrected. "I saw her immediately after her meeting with you, and she didn't look very happy. But she said you were just fine. I didn't hear anything different until she was talking on the phone over lunch and I overheard how you spoke to her."

Of course, that did exactly what my mother wanted it to. It made me feel guilty. Indignation would almost be justified if she had gone and whined to my mother about me. Knowing she had tried to be nice about me, but my mother had heard her talking just made me feel worse.

"I will do my best to be nice or at least not too hard," I promise. "And if I get a chance, I'll apologize for whatever I may have done that upset her. But you do have to understand I was just trying to protect my company."

"You don't need to protect your company from a woman who's trying to drag you kicking and screaming into the new century," she said.

"Funny hearing that from my mother," I pointed out.

"Funny isn't exactly the word I would use," she said. "Something for you to contemplate."

She turned around with a sharp flip of her hair and stalked back to the office building. I couldn't help but laugh. Even when Mom was angry and tough, she managed to amuse me. She was the definition of feisty, and the fact that her marriage to my father had lasted as long as it had was a testament to the characters of both of them. And to the possibility that real love could exist.

I went back to work, determined to bury myself and all the paperwork and messages I had skipped during my vacation, but my mind was elsewhere. Mom's lecture had gotten to me. And quite possibly so had Merry's enormous eyes and sexy smile. For the rest of the day, I ended up spending entirely too much time worrying about how I was going to make it up to the new social media darling.

Those thoughts were still distracting me from getting as much done as I wanted to, and soon nearly everyone else had left the complex. It wasn't uncommon for me to still be working when everybody else was gone and most of the buildings were dark. But that night I was lost in my thoughts and couldn't seem to figure out what to do next. I still hadn't come up with any way to apologize and make my new employee feel better when my brother Vince made the decision about the end of the day for me.

Coming into my office with a giant bag of takeout, he effectively brought my workday to a close.

"Thought I'd find you here," he said. "You've got to pry yourself away from the desk. I know you and I lost a lot of quality time together while you were on vacation, but you can't try to fit it all back in by just staying there overnight," he teased.

"Shut up," I said. "What did you bring?"

"Chicken," he said.

The lights were still on over the patio out back, and the temperature was warm and comfortable, so we brought the food outside rather than settling into the breakroom. He spread out what looked like enough food for about five people. Which meant it was going to be just enough for the two of us. We dove into the fried chicken, biscuits, mashed potatoes, and corn, and talked about the upcoming race season. This was always an exciting time of the year. A fresh season of races stretched in front of us, and everything was electric with possibility and potential. I pointedly didn't mention Merry, even when Vince seemed to try to guide the conversation in that direction and looked at me like he was there for gossip. I wasn't going to take the bait.

6

MERRY

Merry's log. Star date... I didn't know. What did that really mean, anyway? Despite my grandmother's deep devotion to *Star Trek* in all its various iterations, it didn't rub off on me. I might have inherited more of my features and characteristics from her than any other member of my family, but that particular fandom didn't come along with my almond eyes or the weird way my thumbs bent backward. Or the pissed-off determination my grandmother would have referred to as grit but everybody else knows was just stubbornness. Whatever it was and for whatever reason I had it, it was what fueled me the morning of my third day of working for Freeman Racing.

My interaction with Quentin was still bothering me. After all, he wasn't even the one who hired me. He didn't really have any place preemptively evaluating my quality of work or the value of my contribution to his company. Obviously, other people who worked for him, including his mother and brother, believed he was in need of my professional services. So, he should have just accepted their input, respected my qualifications, and given me the space to do my job without already assigning me failures.

Of course, that was also a fairly ridiculous way to look at it. Regardless of who hired me or who within the company thought my skills were going to be beneficial to the company and its success, Quentin owned the company and was the one who ran it. His opinion was actually the only one that really mattered when it came right down to it. He had the ability to decide I wasn't doing well enough or that he didn't need me and just kick me to the curb. I wasn't going to let that happen. As much because I wanted the job and the security that came along with it, his arrogance and assumptions about me made me angry. I didn't like the way he'd treated me from the very beginning and especially didn't like the thought of him just going about his life continuing to think that way. He seemed like one of those people who floated around at the top of every situation he ever encountered. No matter what, if there was a food chain, he was at the head of it and he was comfortable with that.

But I was going to prove him wrong. No matter what I needed to do, I was going to show him his assumptions about me were far off base. Not only was I very good at what I did, but I was going to take that expertise and those skills and use them to whip his company's image into shape. Once he saw what a difference good social media could make, he wouldn't make hair-trigger assumptions about anybody else again. At least not about me.

Before heading into the office, I took a few minutes to go back over all the work I'd compiled the day before. After spending my first day at the complex exploring and getting familiar with the buildings and the people who worked in them, I devoted the next day to creating content plans and schedules. Managing the presence of such a large, dynamic company wasn't as easy as just occasionally throwing a picture up or sharing posts made by fans. It didn't take much digging through the accounts Minnie gave me access to for me at to realize just how extensive the reach of the company was, and how many angles I would have to use to approach the communities that made up the fans.

Rather than just one type of person or one type of fandom, I needed to familiarize myself with the various different people who enjoyed bike racing. From the people who loved the adrenaline and competition of the races themselves, to those more interested in the machines, to the ones who poised themselves as devotees of the riders, there were different fans to appeal to on each platform. There was also the need to reach out to similar-minded people who might become fans of racing simply by being exposed to it.

Add in needing to share schedules for races, build up interest in special events, put out feelers for securing appearances, court potential sponsors, and stimulate revenue streams through exposure to available merchandise, and it was a tremendous undertaking. But one I was ready and willing to do. I had the plans for the next few weeks sketched out along with longer-term projections. I had gone through all the pictures I'd taken on my first day, selected my favorites, and edited them. I had even invested in a large whiteboard I set up in my apartment which I added appropriate hashtags to every time one popped into my head.

I had arms full of materials and a point to make. This was my job, and I wasn't letting him shake me.

The drive from my apartment to the complex was long

enough to let me get pumped up for the coming confrontation. Now that I was aware I didn't have to maintain a formal business appearance when I was in the office, I'd thrown my hair up into a ponytail, slipped on my favorite pair of sunglasses, and had the windows rolled down. It was fortunate the majority of the drive happened along back roads because houses I drove by probably wouldn't be appreciative of the music blaring from my speakers. But the songs energized me and got me ready to make my presentation to Quentin. If he wasn't going to take my word for what I could do, he was going to see the evidence for himself.

By the time I pulled into the parking lot and turned down the music in response to the glare from the guard, I felt ready to face off against the fearless leader of Freeman Racing and secure my spot once and for all. What I wasn't prepared for was the man I actually encountered that morning. I went first to my office so I could drop off what I didn't need for the presentation and get my hair under control before going to his office. Before I could do so, Quentin showed up at my doorway.

He carried with him a cup of coffee and a forced smile, and I tilted my head to the side to look at him, evaluating what exactly was happening.

"May I come in?" he finally asked.

I snapped back into reality and nodded, waving him in.

"Yeah. Sure. Sorry. Of course, come in," I stumbled.

Damn. That was not the impression I wanted to give this morning. The wind in my face and loud music was supposed to make me steady and driven, not stumbling and confused.

Quentin came into the office and turned to close the door behind him. I stood in front of my desk, squared off to him, waiting for whatever was going to come.

"I wanted to apologize for my attitude the other day," he said. "That wasn't the way I should have spoken to you, especially the first time we were meeting. It wasn't fair of me to make assumptions about you, and I'm sorry if I made you feel uncomfortable. I'll be the first to admit social media isn't really my thing. You could probably tell that just by looking at the accounts for the company. I've even tried with my own personal accounts, and I think I might be better at those than I am with the business ones. Probably because I don't have to try to really appeal to anybody. Nobody looks at them but my family, so it's just pictures and things."

I nodded. "That's pretty much how it goes for most people. Personal accounts are easier because you usually don't have to impress people. You're not trying to sell yourself. Hopefully. I mean, I don't really know you. That could be your thing. Trying not to make assumptions."

He scoffed and shook his head. "No. You can assume that all you want. But, like I said, I wasn't really sure what it was all about when my mother suggested I hire a social media consultant. To tell you the truth, I didn't even know that was a thing. So, I'm sorry if I came across however I came across. You do your thing, and I promise I'm not going to get in your way. And I'll help you when I can. Just let me know if there's something you need, and I'll figure it out for you."

I should have responded. There should have been words that came out and continued the conversation, or at least acknowledged what he said. But nothing seemed to be forming in my brain. I stood there just trying to take it all in, processing what just happened. When the words did come, I had to swallow them down and stop myself from gloating about him showing up and all but groveling in front of me.

Instead, I nodded. He stared at me for a second, determined that was all he was going to get from me, and took a step closer to hand me the coffee. I mumbled something that might have been a 'thank you' when I took it, and he offered another tight smile.

When he was gone, I took a sip of the coffee. It was perfect. How did he possibly do that? Staring at the door to my office didn't answer any of my questions, but it gave me a chance to distract myself. After a few seconds, I put the cup down on my desk and dug around in my purse until I found my phone.

Finally, I pulled it out along with one of the granola bars and dropped down into my desk chair. Peeling open the bar and taking a bite, I opened my phone and rattled off a text to my brother. He wasn't going to believe this. For the last two days he'd been listening to me complain about Quentin and building myself up for an epic showdown today. He'd been supportive and reassuring with just enough big-brother protectiveness to make me feel better about the situation. I was glad to be able to tell him things were looking up and he didn't need to worry so much about me.

Sitting at my desk and enjoying my coffee while I scrolled through the news and checked a few of my favorite fluff sites was a reward for coming out on top of the confrontation. Even if there wasn't really a confrontation. That was just a technicality. He'd shown up with a peace offering and apologized.

I totally won.

After my brief celebration, I set the empty coffee cup aside and dove into work. There was a lot to be done even with the elimination of my presentation. The whiteboard would still be beneficial even if I didn't haul it into Quentin's office. Taking out my schedule and prepared content, I posted the first tweets and Instagram posts. Only a few seconds later I noticed they already had likes. When I took a glance at the name on the account that gave the likes, I was glad I wasn't still drinking the coffee. My laugh at seeing they were both from Quentin's personal account definitely wouldn't have kept it in my mouth.

7

QUENTIN

I had always been extremely protective of my company. Saying I was successful and that running the racing company had been my dream my whole life would be a massive understatement. Ever since I was very young, I'd envisioned my future and known I wanted more than just a mediocre life. Not that my family was mediocre or that they didn't put me on a path toward anything more than that. Quite the opposite. My parents are quite possibly the most supportive two human beings to have ever been put on Earth. They always did everything they could to make the four of us feel like we could do everything and anything we wanted. For me, that meant chasing success.

From the time I was about nine or ten, my focus had been zeroed in on bike racing. I'd always been in love with the sport. The power and beauty of the machines. The thrill and adrenaline of watching a race. The constant energy and drive to get better. It was something I knew I wanted to be a part of, and my sights were set on not only doing it but being successful at it. That meant after I achieved it, I didn't want anything to happen that might threaten it.

That included having new people around. Over the years my team had grown from just my family to including several other people, but each of them had gone through a period when I had to get to know them, get accustomed to having them around. In some cases, it took months for me to feel really used to having them there and comfortable with having them be a part of various aspects of the company.

Somehow it wasn't like that with Merry. Very quickly, I settled into a routine with her. It only took a few days after that fairly disastrous first meeting when my defensiveness reared its head in a very big way for me to be used to her being around. My daily routine and habits even adapted to her being around without me realizing it. It wasn't until the middle of her second week that I really caught myself adjusting my usual schedule because of her.

I was sitting in my office, eating lunch at my desk as I frequently did, and pulled up the company's Twitter on my phone. As I ate, I scrolled through what she had done and clicked the heart icon beneath the newest post. Then I went through the pictures she took and retweeted them. They were images of the complex, and I was damn proud of them. But after I did it, I realized just how out of character that was. Not only had I willingly and purposely hit a little heart icon, something I'd only done the day I apologized to her so she would see I was engaging with what she was doing, but I crossed my platforms.

My personal social media was rarely used except to check in with old friends. They were used to not seeing new posts from me and getting only the occasional brief comment or response from me. But there I was, retweeting images of the complex she took. It came as a surprise to me, considering it wasn't exactly a secret how I felt about social media in general.

Despite those personal feelings, I'd learned to appreciate, at least to a degree, that social media was important for my company. It was the way of the future. Well, actually, according to Darren, it was the way of the future ten years ago, which meant it was the way of the past and the current, but I was catching up.

I had gotten used to having Merry as part of the company but rarely actually saw her. Except for in passing, we didn't see each other during the day. But I figured that was actually a benefit during this early time in us working together. The less frequently I saw her, the less chance I had to stick my foot in my mouth again. And the less time I had to spend training my brain to stay professional.

That day, however, I knew I had to break the routine and personally go to talk to her. The first race was coming up quickly, and I assumed she would want to feature it heavily in upcoming posts. I wanted to find out how much help she would need from me to get the pictures and information needed to make the posts as effective as possible. And I wanted that conversation to happen with me. She and Darren were getting pretty chummy. Several of the times I caught a glimpse of her over the last week she was right there along with my youngest brother, talking and laughing, seeming completely comfortable and at ease with him. And I hated to admit that something about that fact didn't sit right with me.

While it might have been easier for me to just let him handle the conversation with her about the social media campaigns, there was no way I was going to let that happen. She was hired for *my* company and was creating these campaigns for *me*, not him. I wanted to be the one to work with her, to get that chance to interact with her. In the back of my mind, I knew that reaction was ridiculous. There was no reason I should be even thinking about how much time she was spending with my brother or what they were talking about. It shouldn't matter to me how she was getting to know the others in the company. If I was going to think about her relationships with other people in the complex at all, I should be happy she was making friends and feeling at ease. A happy employee was a productive and loyal employee.

And yet, here I was. Merry obviously wasn't trying to make me feel jealous. She never did anything that seemed she was trying to catch my attention and force it onto her interaction with my brother, and he never said anything that implied anything about them that was more than just another coworker. But there was still a twinge when I thought of her and when I saw them together. It was stupid, but I had no control over it.

That might have been what bothered me more than anything. Control was an important thing to me. I liked to control as many aspects of my life as humanly possible, and that definitely applied to my work. Not being able to control how I felt about my social media consultant being friendly with my brother was uncomfortable and strange. Coming up on the first race of the season was stressful enough as it was. I didn't need the additional stress and pressure of a new team member not sticking to the script and keeping up with my expectations.

But, again, that really wasn't Merry's fault. She didn't know the expectations, and she wasn't familiar with what I saw as the company's set way of operating. She wasn't doing anything wrong or purposely trying to get a rise out of me. I would just have to keep reminding myself of that. I went over that several times in my mind as I made my way through the building to her office. She was sitting behind her desk, picking her way through a selection of chopped fruit in a clear plastic bowl in front of her as she leaned over her tablet.

"Don't you think it would be easier to use a laptop?" I asked.

Merry jumped slightly and looked up at me. She smiled through swallowing a large chunk of pineapple she'd popped in her mouth just as I walked into the room.

"No," she said. "I like looking at it like this. Most of the time people aren't going to be looking at social media on their computers. I mean, they definitely do, but if they're out and about, they're going to have their phone or a tablet. So, I make sure to check the mobile view and what it looks like on different devices."

"It's different?" I asked.

That was probably a stupid question considering she had literally just explained to me it was.

"Yes," Merry said matter-of-factly.

I nodded through an awkward silence.

"Well, I came by to tell you we're having a team meeting, and I want to make sure you're there. There are some changes coming up for this season, and I want you to stay in the loop so you can keep everything updated," I said.

"Sure," she told me. I stared at her with expectation, and her mouth fell open slightly. "Oh. Now?"

"Yeah. I was actually headed that way," I said.

"Oh. Sorry. Yeah, let me grab my things."

She sounded flustered, which I thought was cute in spite of myself. Merry gathered a few things and followed me out of the office. We walked in silence to the meeting room, and when we got there, the rest of the team was already in place.

"All right," I said, walking to the head of the table and

setting the folder I was holding down in front of me. "The first race is right around the corner, and now it's time to really buckle down and get ready for the season. I want this to be the best one yet, and that's going to require hard work from all of us. To that end, I want to talk about the changes to the team. Greg and Darren will both be racing this season. That's an exciting development for all of us, and I'm really looking forward to seeing how the dynamic plays out. But it's important everyone realizes this will mean we need all hands on deck."

As we talked about the coming season and how we were going to manage having two riders in the races, I glanced over at Merry. I had expected that she wouldn't know what we were talking about and would probably be confused, but I immediately noticed she was taking notes on her tablet. It made me even more sure of her work ethic, and I liked that. As the meeting broke up, I took a step toward her.

"Merry, could you stay after for just a bit?" I asked. "I want to discuss everything with you one-on-one."

Her eyes widened slightly, but she nodded.

8

MERRY

"Sure, no problem."

I wasn't sure how I was supposed to react when Quentin asked me to stay after the team meeting to talk with him. My brain went in several different directions and couldn't figure out which one to settle on.

I figured it was a good thing that he was asking me to come to the team meeting. Even if seeing him at the door to my office put more butterflies in my stomach than I would want to admit to. He was my boss.

I had no business thinking he was as stupidly hot as I thought he was. I'd hoped having that sort of response to him it was just a primal, snap sort of reaction that happened because I wasn't expecting it.

At least, that's what I told myself. I tried to convince myself it would go away, that I would get used to him and soon he would just be another guy working at the complex. Or my brain would wrap itself around the fact that he was my boss and I couldn't have that attraction to him. But that hadn't happened yet. Two weeks after starting at Freeman Racing, I was still deep in the throes of thinking the owner of the company was absurdly attractive. Not that I could or would do anything about it, but it constantly hung over me.

I wasn't sure I was ready to be alone with him again. It wasn't just the intense and inappropriate attraction. Quentin still intimidated me. I wasn't going to admit that, of course, but the idea of working one-on-one with him made my stomach do flips. But I managed to keep that to myself. No matter what was going on in my mind or how I was feeling about him and being alone in a room with him, I was going to woman up and do my job.

If I pushed aside all of the inconvenient and awkward feelings and emotions going through me, I was actually looking forward to working directly with Quentin and finding out more about the upcoming race. I was excited about seeing my first bike race and finally finding out what all the hype was about. In just the short time I had been managing the social media accounts for the company, I'd learned the fans were truly devoted. I might go so far as to say some were rabid. The races obviously stirred something up in them, and I was excited to find out what that was.

But there was a lot of work to do before that race came. I had been working on coming up with more ideas on how to ramp up the social media platforms and make them more interesting and appealing. I knew if I did it right, we could pack the stands with even more fans and get them riled up and excited about supporting both Greg and Darren. After everybody left, Quentin looked at me and gestured to one of the chairs closer to him.

"Thanks for staying. I haven't had much of a chance to work directly with you, and I wanted to check in with how everything is progressing. Especially with the first race coming up, I want to make sure we're on the same page," he said.

"Everything is going great," I told him. "I was actually planning on trying to find a time to meet up with you at this week to go over my plans. So, this is perfect."

"Great. Why don't we sit down and go over what you're thinking, and we'll see if there's anything we can tighten up or change..." He hesitated. "Not that I think you aren't doing your job or that I'm going to tell you how to do it or anything."

I shook my head. "I get it."

We both let out awkward, somewhat uncomfortable laughs and sat down. I was glad I'd thought to grab my messenger bag and was able to take out files with printouts of my plans. Spreading them out on the table, I started going over them, explaining each approach and how I intended on scheduling the posts and encouraging interaction with followers. Quentin listened with much more attention and interest than I expected him to, even giving insights and suggestions as we went.

"I think you understand social media better than you think you do," I told him after a particularly good suggestion that had me rethinking an entire day of posts.

"Maybe we won't go that far. But I'm starting to get a hold of it a little better," he admitted.

Before I could say anything else, my stomach made a loud rumbling sound. I laughed and looked down at the time. I hadn't realized we had been sitting there for more than an hour already.

"Apparently I'm hungry," I said.

"Apparently." My stomach growled again, and he laughed.

"All right, all right, I believe you," he said.

I started gathering all the papers from the table. "Why don't we leave this for now and pick it up again later? It's getting late. Everybody is probably gone by now. I know you don't want to keep hanging out here talking about this stuff into the night."

"Do you have somebody waiting for you at home?" he asked.

My mouth fell open slightly, and I looked over at him. "What?"

"I just meant you seem eager to rush off. I was just wondering if that's because you have somebody you want to get home to," he clarified.

The heat coming up on my cheeks embarrassed me even more, but I covered it by looking into my bag like I was checking for something.

"No," I told him. "No one at home waiting for me. I just figured you spend so much time around here as it is, you wouldn't want to be kept here all night going over stuff you don't like anyway. I can just bring all your comments and suggestions home with me, work on it some more, and we'll meet up again."

"Like I said, I'm getting used to the social media stuff. And I'm seeing how important it truly is to our brand. Why don't we just order some dinner and keep going?" he suggested. "I mean, if you're okay with that?"

Before I even responded, he'd pulled out his phone and dialed a number that seemed extremely familiar to him. I had the feeling this was not the first time he had called that particular number to bring food to the office.

Half an hour later, he left the meeting room to meet with the delivery driver and came back with two huge bags of food. He spread out a pile of individually wrapped street-style tacos, chips, and guacamole, then went to the break-room and came back with drinks. The food smelled incredible, and it took all the control I could muster not to just throw myself headlong into the pile and eat my way out. I did manage to keep my composure and selected only one of the tacos. But I couldn't hold back the groan when I took my first bite.

"Good?" Quentin asked.

"It's delicious," I told him.

"My favorite restaurant for takeout," he said. "More often than not, if I'm here at the office late and want some dinner, this is what I'm getting."

"I can see why. It's a good choice," I told him.

We looked over at each other, and I felt another flutter. Dragging my eyes away from him, I took another massive bite of taco to distract me and went back to rambling about the plans. It was a pleasant surprise that while Quentin clearly wasn't going to become a social media convert anytime soon, he was open to what I had to say and accepted it was going to work for him. By the time we finished eating and had gone over everything several times, I felt one hundred percent more comfortable with him and with our working relationship. Maybe it really was possible for us to get along and to work together effectively.

I left the office three hours later than I usually would, which meant my phone was already blowing up when I got to my car.

"Where have you been?" my best friend, Olivia, demanded when I answered.

"Working," I told her. "Like a responsible adult."

"Do you realize what time it is?" she asked.

"I know. There was a meeting that ran late. I'll meet you at the bar. Be there soon."

Olivia and I had made plans to meet up a few days before, but I'd honestly forgotten about it when Quentin asked if someone was home waiting for me. The question was so unexpected, and it seemed so personal it made my mind go blank. But as soon as I saw her name on my phone, the plans popped back into my head and I felt guilty for keeping her waiting. It had been a while since the two of us had a chance to hang out together. Olivia had been off on a trip with her parents spending time with her family before school started up again. She was a high school art teacher who had me in constant awe.

We met up at a bar near my apartment, and I found her already sitting at a table with two beers and a massive plate of nachos. I dropped down into the seat across from her and took a swig of my beer.

"That kind of day?" Olivia asked.

I eyed the nachos, thinking about the tacos I'd eaten with Quentin not too long before.

"Long couple of weeks," I said.

She wrapped her hand around her beer, and I knew she was prepared. I dove in and told her all about my new job, the complex, and, maybe especially, Quentin.

9

QUENTIN

When I had looked for a plot of land to build my house on, I had purposefully chosen one with a good amount of distance from neighbors. I worked in a loud and often chaotic business and when I was home, I wanted peace and quiet.

The longer I lived in the house, however, I realized the real benefit of not living close to neighbors wasn't for me, it was for those potential neighbors. As I stood in the kitchen putting together a platter of snacks, I cringed at the loud voices coming through the sliding doors from the backyard. I didn't understand how my three brothers and my parents could manage to sound like a frat party, especially considering the sound had to come up a flight of steps and across a large deck to get in the kitchen.

It was family night, and as usual, everyone was gathered at my house. I loved having them there. Really, I did. But that night I was having trouble settling into the relaxation and enjoyment of just spending time with them. My nerves felt frazzled and worn, and stress and anxiety were pumping along my veins. It wasn't a completely foreign feeling. With the first race of the season coming up, I anticipated being somewhat off my game. I always felt a bit on edge before a race, especially the first race of the season, was coming up. As much as I loved the racing industry and thrived on the adrenaline and fun of races, there was the unavoidable stress and anticipation that came along with them.

This season, I was going to be worried about Greg as well as Darren. Whenever races were looming, I started thinking about everything that could happen, all the logistics that had to fall into place to make sure the race went smoothly and safely. By the time the race came, I'd have worried myself out and would be ready to just kick back and have a good time, but that was still a bit away.

But this time it was different. Usually having a family night would reduce my stress and make me feel better. Spending time with my brothers and my parents always helped to ease anxiety.

That wasn't happening that night. Having them around not only wasn't making me feel better, but it seemed to be pushing me further and I hated that.

Carrying the plate of snacks and two beers, I walked out of my house and headed down to the fire burning in the yard below. The temperature was sticky and hot that day, without even a slight breeze to break it up. Not my usual summer evening I enjoyed so much. I had brought down deck chairs and set them up further away from the flames so the heat was less intense. I sat down and set the beers and snacks on a folding table beside me. Taking a deep swig of the beer, I watched the flames jump in front of me, hoping something would click in my head and I'd get out of the funk I was feeling.

A few minutes later, Nick came up and took the chair

next to me. He followed my stare and looked into the flames for a few seconds before turning back to me. I continued to ignore my brother, really not feeling like talking. To one side, the other two brothers were playing lawn darts in a way I was fairly certain would result in an emergency room visit, and to the other, my parents were pretending to be casual and not worrying about their grown sons, but occasionally shouting at them to be careful. I didn't want to deal with any of it and stayed quiet. Maybe if I just stayed that way for long enough, Nick would get the hint and leave me alone. It wasn't that I necessarily wanted my family away from the house, but I also wasn't feeling especially social.

I should have known better. Nick was the closest to me of my three brothers, and he could always tell when something was bothering me. He was also always the first one to ask me about it. The others might try to be subtle and give me space, but not Nick. He had absolutely no qualms about prying into my thoughts, which was exactly what he did then.

"Penny for your thoughts, old man?" he asked.

It was a joke we'd carried on between us from the time I was a teenager. I was never shy about pointing out the privileges that came along with me being the oldest. I had a later curfew, got to drive first, had the first girlfriend of the brothers. But it didn't take long for Nick to take that and turn it into taunting me about being old. That only got worse when I dedicated myself to the company. According to him, the work made me stuffy and inflexible, a grumpy old man before my time. He appointed himself officially responsible for cutting through the grump. Usually he could. But that night I didn't even know where to start.

"If I knew what was up, I'd tell you," I said and took another sip of my beer.

Nick tilted his head to the side like he was trying to look directly into my face, but I didn't turn to look at him.

"What do you mean?" he asked. "Something's obviously up."

I shrugged, letting out a breath.

"Feeling antsy, I guess. It's probably just the first race coming up. You know how I get," I said, hoping that would be enough to convince Nick to drop the conversation.

Even as I was saying it, though, I knew that wasn't really what was going on. At least, that wasn't all of it. There was more, I just didn't know exactly what. I couldn't put it into words. I got a brief flash of lush hips and a distracting smile, but I ruthlessly shoved it down, swallowing it and chasing it with a guzzle of beer. I couldn't let myself think that way. It wasn't about her. I couldn't let it be about Merry.

"Yeah, I know how you get, but this is different," Nick pointed out. I still didn't respond, and he gave a relenting nod.

He reached over me and grabbed a handful of the snacks I'd brought out. Still staring at me, he popped a few in his mouth and chewed. I slid my eyes over to him.

"Enjoying that?" I asked.

"Yes," he said without hesitation. I turned back to the fire, and he leaned closer. "You'd tell me if it was something else, right? Like if you were in trouble or sick or something, yeah?"

His voice had dropped to a lower, softer tone like he was trying to stop it from carrying over to our parents or brothers. He was genuinely worried about me, wanting to make sure I was all right but wanting to keep it between us. I nodded. Even without words, that seemed like enough for Nick, and he sat back in his chair. We sat there silently for a few more minutes, watching the fire and drinking our beer.

When Darren and Vince finally gave up on their game and dropped down in other chairs on the opposite side of the fire, Nick got up. He crossed over to them, and I heard him start talking to Vince about the stock market. That was their thing. I'd never gotten into the stock market, though I had some investments a firm managed for me. But the two of them seemed to think of it as another sport.

I didn't really care what they were talking about. As much as I didn't want to admit it even to myself, and never would have said it to Nick, I was relieved when he walked away and left me alone again. It was a disquieting, upsetting feeling. I loved hanging out with my brothers, so I wished I knew what was going on now to make me want to just be alone. The thought went through my head that I should call Cole, but I knew my best friend had been dealing with his own shit recently. I didn't want to drag him down further. At the same time, maybe that's what we both needed. Just some time away from everything. A night at the batting cages like the old days, smashing the hell out of baseballs and being far too loud and inappropriate, sounded like exactly what I needed. That would shake me out of whatever was going on in my head.

I made a mental note to give him a call after the first race was done and find a time when we could get together.

•

10

MERRY

It was finally the day of my first race. That wasn't a sentiment I ever thought would go through my mind. It was finally beach day, sure. It was finally the first day of vacation, yes. It was finally the day I was going to sit around in my sweatpants and eat obscene amounts of popcorn, absolutely. But the concept of being excited for a race of any kind was pretty much foreign.

Yet, I'd gotten to that place. I was genuinely excited when I woke up knowing it was the day we'd been building up to, the day we'd finally get out onto the track. Those thoughts went through my mind as I ate a bowl of cereal, my hair a mess, and my bathrobe far from work attire, and I realized how silly I must sound. I'd worked for Freeman Racing for less than a month, yet I was already bundling myself in with the rest of them as if I was some sort of integral part of the process and had any ownership at all over the win or loss. As if the work I did for their social media had become a critical element of their functioning.

Maybe that was actually it. I was just so damn good at my job, I'd gotten myself wrapped up in the energy of it.

After all, that was a big part of the purpose of social media for something like a racing company. It wasn't just about making sure the fans knew when the events were and how to buy tickets or giving them glimpses of the bikes and the tracks. It was about sweeping them up in the furor and making them feel like a part of the team. Giving them a sense of involvement and belonging created excitement and fostered a sense of loyalty. They were much more likely to want to attend multiple races, buy merchandise, and even pay for special events and appearances if they felt like they were some sort of insider who had a true connection.

That made a lot more sense than to think somehow in the last couple of weeks I'd developed a true interest in racing. Except as I got ready that morning, dressing in jeans and a Freeman Racing T-shirt rather than a dress and winding my hair up into a bun on the back of my head rather than styling it or having it hang down, I realized I really was excited. I was truly looking forward to the experience. And I actually did feel like part of the team.

That was certainly unexpected. But not unwelcome.

As soon as I got to the complex, I could feel the energy and excitement buzzing in the air. It was usually far quieter and calmer than I think most people would assume a race company would be, but that morning it was everything I envisioned it might be. People rushing around, noise and chaos, trucks lined up everywhere. There were more people than I was used to seeing in the complex, and even as I tried to identify all of them, I realized I didn't know who most of them were or what role they played in the spectacle.

Not wanting to get in the way but wanting to capture as much of it as possible, I stood off to the side and watched the preparations unfold. Men brought bikes, tools, and equipment from the storage sheds and workshops and loaded them up on the haulers. Others secured them in place and checked to make sure everything was safe and ready for the trip. I noticed a few people on phones as they ran around, making arrangements and checking details, but I didn't know what they were talking about.

I'd captured several dozen pictures when Glenda came up to stand beside me. Even the receptionist looked bright-eyed and excited when I smiled over at her.

"Happy race day," she said.

I grinned wider. "Happy race day. You seem excited."

"Always am. Race day is fun. Well, race day is a lot of stress and anxiety and causes everybody to go just a little bit out of their minds, but it can also be fun," she added.

"This is my first one. Tell me about it. What does everybody do? What's all this stuff? How does everybody handle it?" I asked.

I wanted to whip out my tablet and use the voice recording app I sometimes used to keep notes for myself, but that might seem like I was drifting too close to pretending I was an investigative reporter. I needed to calm down and listen and gather up what I could to incorporate into posts later. Glenda exuded energy as she described the usual race day to me and told me about little rituals and traditions they had. She sounded like she knew them all so well and had such affection for them. It was touching to see how much care she had for the entire thing. I really liked Glenda. She was sharp, smart, and funny when she wanted to be, and tight, controlled, and no-nonsense when she needed to be. That seemed like the exact woman suited to hold down the desk at Freeman Racing.

"Everything ready to go?" one of the men called out to the others just as she finished.

"Packed up and ready," another replied.

I turned to Glenda.

"I better go find Minnie. I haven't even checked in with her yet, and I want to make sure there's nothing special I need to know before we head to the track," I told her.

She waved and I rushed off to find the Freeman matriarch. She was coming out of the office building just as I ran toward it. I stopped in front of her, and she grinned.

"Merry, I was just looking for you," she said.

"You were?" I asked. "I was looking for you. I'm sorry I didn't let you know I was here. I got wrapped up in watching them pack everything up and lost track of time. Do I need to know anything specific before I go to the track? Do I need special credentials or anything?"

"They won't be necessary," she told me.

"Oh," I said, hoping I was doing a good enough job of concealing my disappointment.

I'd been hoping I was going to have the opportunity to be right down there in the action with the team. Not only would it let me capture some amazing pictures, it would give me the most authentic experience. But now it seemed like I was being relegated to the general admission area at best, and the backstage area at worst.

"They won't question you when they see you're with me," Minnie said.

"With you?" I asked, not sure what she meant.

"Yes. I came looking for you because I want to invite you to ride with me to the track," she said.

"I would love that," I told her, feeling relieved and happy.

She gestured for me to follow her, and we went to the parking lot where she'd parked. I wasn't going to say anything about it, but there was an element of surprise that she didn't have a driver bringing her around. With as much money and wealth as Quentin had, I just assumed they would have a luxurious lifestyle. But when I really thought about it, Minnie didn't seem like the kind of woman who would want to be chauffeured everywhere all the time. She'd want the freedom, the ability to just jump into her car and go where she wanted to go.

"My husband is already at the track with the boys," she explained when we climbed into her car. "They always want to get a really early start on race days. But I'm not one for hanging around there while they do practice laps and stress over every little detail. Too much for me. I'd rather come here and supervise."

She laughed and we pulled out of the parking lot, headed toward the track behind the caravan of trucks.

"What's it like having four sons?" I asked. "That must have been a lot while they were growing up."

"In a lot of different ways," Minnie said with a laugh. "But they were worth every single moment of it. You know, you're far from the first person to say it must have been a lot to raise four boys."

"I'm sorry," I said, suddenly uncomfortable and worried I'd somehow offended her. "I just meant..."

"No, I know," she said. "I understand where you're coming from. Boys can be loud and rambunctious and messy. But it's not like I had four of the same out-of-control creature running around my house all the time." She laughed. "That might have pushed me over the edge. They were fairly well spread out in age, so that helped. But they are also just so different. There are some things about them that are the same, of course. They're brothers. They aren't going to be but so completely different."

I listened as she told me about her sons, listing out all the ways they were different and all the ways they were the same, frequently attributing the characteristics to either herself or her husband. Some of the things I heard were surprising, while others just made me more curious. I liked Darren, the youngest of the brothers a lot, but wasn't familiar with the other two. As far as I knew, Nick didn't play an active role in the company, and I wondered why. But it was Quentin who was the real wild card.

Quentin and I were working better together, but it hadn't taken away my questions and anxiety. I still wasn't sure if he thought I was doing a consistently good job or not. He rarely gave feedback, and when he did, it was mostly things he wanted me to include or just a brief like on the social media platforms. Of course, that drove me insane. I was still out to impress him and wanted him to think I was doing well. Even if I didn't want to admit that out loud to myself much less to anyone else. Minnie didn't give me much insight into Quentin or what he might think of me. She told me about when he was a little boy and his relationships with his brothers, but little about him as a man. It meant I was still going to have to figure it out on my own.

When we got to the track, Minnie gave me a quick overview of everything, and then we parted ways. She was going straight for the team, but I needed some general pictures and wanted to talk to the organizers a bit. This was much more of an undertaking than I expected. When Minnie described the track and surrounding facilities, she didn't give me an accurate perspective of scale, so what I thought was a quaint little event space turned out to be a sprawling complex that rivaled Freeman Racing but had none of the grass or trees. That meant by the time I found the private booth where I was going to sit, my feet were aching. Sighing with relief, I sat down and relaxed for a few moments, enjoying the cool of the shade and not being on my feet.

Finally, I pulled out my phone and posted some of the pictures I'd taken, along with a video I'd made and some of the written content I'd prepared. I did it as fast as I could, not wanting to miss any of the race. A few minutes later, Minnie joined me in the box, squeezing my hand and giving a slight squeal of excitement as she pointed over toward where the riders were readying themselves. Darren waved at us with a bright smile, and I waved back, laughing at the sheer excitement on his face.

The race itself was insane, more than I ever could have imagined. I wasn't prepared for the sound or the smell or the intensity. But I also wasn't prepared for how much I'd love the way it felt running through my veins and pumping in my heart. Not long into the race, I was on my feet, and when Darren came in first, Minnie and I were screaming and jumping up and down, clutching at each other as we cheered.

It was incredible, and I did my best to get as much of it as I could on camera. I looked forward to reviewing everything and pulling out the perfect moments to share.

11

QUENTIN

I was beyond pumped, already jumping up and down and screaming when the bikes were taking their last bank around the curve of the track. Darren was up at the front of the pack, his incredible performance keeping him ahead through the majority of the race. He was nothing short of driven. It was obvious how much energy and time he had put not only into improving his bike, practicing and increasing his focus before the first race. It had paid off in a major way, and I shouted out an excited celebratory as he pulled across the finish line first. I couldn't have asked for a better performance from him. It was inspiring to see his dedication and performance, pulling in the first win of the season. That set the precedent and the tone for us. Now the other racers not only saw his impressive skill and newly redesigned and improved bike but already felt a step behind him. It was a psychological element that could be highly beneficial in the races to come.

The thrill of seeing Darren come in first was so high I almost forgot Greg was in the race as well and stopped paying attention. I was so accustomed to only having my brother representing the company, I was just about to turn around to the rest of the team when I caught sight of Greg's bike dart over the line just a fraction of an instant after the second bike. My cheering became even louder, and I grabbed onto the crew member beside me, shaking him and thumping him on the back. He laughed and returned the pat, joining me in celebrating the tremendous showing for the company.

"Can you believe that?" I shouted over the chaos of the crowd erupting at the end of the race.

"Yes," he shouted back. "This team is badass."

"Hell yeah, it is!"

I couldn't have asked for a better night. We placed ridiculously well in the race, the team was in tremendous spirits, and I knew Merry was there. Even though I didn't see her during the race, knowing she was there watching gave me a boost. It was her first race, and she'd expressed how excited she was to experience it. I couldn't wait to find out what she thought and see if she got any good pictures. This was definitely something I wanted to share with anyone who might happen by our social media.

We took off toward the finish line, and my heart warmed when my baby brother came running toward me to jump into my arms. I grabbed him in a tight hug, and we jumped up and down a few times, laughing and cheering. It wasn't his first win, but every win was exciting, and to land the first of the season was especially thrilling. The season was already off to an amazing start, and I was more revved up than ever for the rest of it.

"Come on, everybody," I called out to the crew. "Let's get cleaned up and head out for some drinks."

"You're going to help clean up?" Greg asked with a mock expression of shock on his face.

I nudged him playfully, and we went about cleaning up our area and loading all the equipment up on the trucks. When we were finished, I directed them to a local bar, promising to meet them there. They deserved it. Hell, we all deserved it after that showing. It might not seem like it to the casual observer or fan, but a massive amount of work went into getting ready for these races. And it was going to take just as much work to get ready for the next one. But that was going to wait. Come the next day, it was back to the grind and seeing what we could do to make our first place lead even bigger and take hold of second place as well. But for tonight, we were going to get out, let loose, and have some fun.

We finished loading up, and I headed away from the track toward my car. Ahead of me I caught sight of Mom and Merry walking alongside each other, talking animatedly. They glanced up and noticed me. I waved and they both waved back enthusiastically, grins stretching across both their faces. Seeing that made me smile even wider and a brighter happiness spread through me. It was awesome seeing them so happy, and it made the night even better. I didn't let myself dwell on why.

"How was your first race?" I asked as I approached the women.

"Amazing," Merry said.

"Merry sat with me in the company box," Mom told me. "She was very enthusiastic."

Both women laughed, and I felt like I was missing something but didn't really mind. It was cute to see them giggling together and having something they shared. Eventually I'd probably hear the story at one of the family bonfires, anyway.

"Glad to hear it. Did you get any good pictures?" I asked.

Merry nodded.

"I mean, I haven't had a chance to really look through all of them, yet. But the ones I glanced at were really good, and I think I got some great video footage, too. I'll post some tomorrow, and the rest I'll send to you so you can see them," she said.

"Sounds great. Well, we're heading to the bar. You're coming, right?"

I made it a point to look at both of them so neither would notice me giving more attention to Merry. They both nodded.

When I got to the bar, it was already crowded and loud. The energy was pulsing through the space, and I immediately got swept up in the atmosphere. The team cheered when they saw I'd gotten there, and I waved my hands above my head to acknowledge all of them.

"I've got the first round," Vince announced.

I often wondered why he wasn't more involved in the racing company than he was. He loved the races and made suggestions here and there, but that was as far as his involvement went. He gathered up the beers the bartender filled and lined up on the bar, handing them out to the team gathered around him. Darren took his pint and climbed up on the nearest table. Holding his hand out over the crowd, he commanded their attention.

"I just want to say a few words," he called out. "Tonight was one of the best of my life. I'm pumped to have come in first, but I know I couldn't have done it without the most amazing team in the industry." He paused to let the crew cheer and shout for a few seconds. "I also want to congratulate Greg on his awesome first race. Coming in third is fucking awesome, and I can't wait to see what else he's going to be able to do. Congratulations, dude. If nothing else, having you out there is going to make me a better racer because I'm not going to be able to let up when I know you're right on my ass trying to take my place."

Everybody laughed and we did a few toasts. A few of them guzzled down the beer and headed for the bar for another round. The bartender already looked thrilled. He knew his pockets were going to be lined with fat tips by the end of the night. Especially since I was there.

But no matter how much I ended up dropping, I intended on having only one beer that night. There was still a half-hour drive ahead of me to get back to the complex, and then I had to unload everything and get it put away. Considering how fast most of the others on the team were pounding back the beers, it seemed I was probably going to be handling most of that on my own. The rideshares around town were going to be doing bang-up business when this was all said and done. Gauging by how things were going, it would probably be around three in the morning by the time I got home at this point.

Feeling the rumble in my stomach that reminded me I hadn't eaten much that day, I headed up to the bar to order some snacks. Greg came up beside me, and I patted him on the back.

"Enjoying your celebration?" I asked.

"Absolutely," he told me. "I could definitely get used to this."

"Well, if you keep on performing like that, you'll have the chance to," I replied. "You had a great run today. Keep it up."

"That's the plan," he said with a smile.

A short-order cook came out of the kitchen carrying a basket of fries in one hand and one of mozzarella sticks in the other. I grabbed both of them and gave a nod toward Greg.

"Relax and enjoy yourself. We're not going to be getting started at work until after lunch tomorrow. Spread it around," I announced, lifting my voice above the loud music now blaring over the speakers.

Greg grinned and nodded happily before disappearing into the crowd. The late start was going to make sure I at least got a little bit of sleep after all this, but it was also just so everybody could kick back and have fun rather than worrying about having to get into the office early the next morning. They deserved to celebrate and then get some much-needed rest.

Carrying the food with me, I crossed the bar, greeting and congratulating members of the team as I went. There were a few other crews there, and I made a point to talk to the riders. Having a competitive spirit was one thing, but there was no point in bitter rivalry. We all loved the same sport, and there was no telling how we might cross paths down the line. Events, autograph signings, and exhibitions often featured multiple teams and could be a boon for anyone involved. I liked to be a good sport, even if the others didn't always follow suit.

When I got through the main crush of people in the middle of the bar, I caught sight of my mother coming out of the restroom. She came up and gave me a quick hug, then led me toward the booths along the back wall. Merry and my dad were sitting across the table from each other but leaned close as they chatted. It seemed like an odd pairing, but they were getting along famously as Merry flipped through images on her tablet. She pointed at the screen and looked at Dad. They laughed together and I smiled as I made it up to the booth.

"What's so funny?" I asked.

I wasn't sure where to sit, but Mom made the decision for me, sliding into place next to Dad. I sat beside Merry, worn-out and happy, if feeling slightly awkward being so close to her while my mind went through a series of emotions.

"Merry was just showing me why she takes so many pictures of everything," Dad said.

"Oh?" I asked, setting the food down in the middle of the table so everyone could share.

"Things like this," Merry said.

She turned the tablet toward me to show off a hilarious image of Darren's face. It looked like he had just swallowed a bug and was falling off his bike at the same time. As far as I knew, neither of those had happened during the race, which somehow made the picture even funnier.

"I guess you don't always get the cover shot first, huh?" I asked.

"Not even close," Merry agreed, pulling the tablet back and flipping through a few more images. "Usually there's one out of every ten or twenty that's good enough to actually post."

"Have you chosen the ones you're going to use?" I asked.

"Some of them. I'm still searching for one that will be perfect for announcing the big win. This is a great chance to really boost followers and get people engaged with your new social media. If we can get this post to go viral, it would be huge," she said.

I sat back and ate, listening to her and Dad talk about

strategies, surprised at how much he seemed to know. Merry reached over and grabbed a mozzarella stick, and I found a strange amount of satisfaction in her casual enjoyment of it. She was really settling in and becoming one of the team.

12

MERRY

I wasn't really intending on staying out late after the race. When I heard they were all going out to grab a couple of drinks and celebrate the amazing showing of the team, I couldn't reject the invitation to go along. It would seem rude and like I was trying to avoid them. Besides, I wanted to be accepted by them and feel like a real part of the team. It meant a lot to me when Minnie asked me to sit with her, and I was so pumped full of adrenaline and excitement I knew I couldn't just go home and settle down for the night. I would just go to the bar, have one beer, say my congratulations, then bow out and head home to be a responsible professional.

But then Quentin spread the news he wasn't expecting anybody to show up to work the next day until after lunch. That gave me some extra wiggle room. I could grab a few extra hours of rest and be freshened up and ready to go. Which meant I could hang out for a little longer. That turned into getting into a deep conversation with Gus Freeman about the company's social media and my approach. To say I was surprised at how interested he seemed to be would be an understatement. For all the resistance his oldest son showed, this man was fascinated and ready to be a part of the process. He listened to me explain the ins and outs of everything I was doing with the company, showed me his own personal platforms, and offered me suggestions from a fan's perspective.

Those were possibly the most surprising. I would have thought what he had to offer would be pretty much the same as what Quentin and I had already talked about. But I quickly learned that while Quentin's insights were valuable, many of them were definitely coming from the place of the owner of the company. There was a business slant to them, somewhat of a distance. Gus, though deeply involved in the company, was technically retired. He didn't spend nearly as much time around the complex as his wife and sons and didn't have the kind of stakes Quentin did. He was still very much a fan of racing and was able to let me see the postings through those eyes. It helped me to clarify my focus and figure out what pictures, videos, and captions to use to appeal to the full demographic.

Which, of course, meant I went from one beer to two, bottomed out the basket of fries and went for another, and was lingering at the bar far later than I expected to be. The numbers glowing on my phone read two-thirty when I finally stumbled into my apartment. A key that already tended to be a bit sticky and temperamental was obnoxious as hell through my fog and exhaustion, but I finally managed to wrestle the door open and make my way inside. I dropped my purse and bag to the floor and peeled off my shoes, kicking them to the side. Just lifting my foot that way made me wobble, and I was glad for the rideshare Minnie had arranged to bring me home. It was going to be inconvenient and annoying to have to shell out the cash and listening to a driver make awkward small talk on the way to the office the next day, but it got me back to the apartment after the bar. That was the top priority for the night.

Right up there with figuring out who the hell was sleeping on my couch.

I crossed the dark living room toward the lump covered with my favorite chenille throw. I was just contemplating whether I should be afraid or not when I got close enough to realize it was my brother. He hadn't told me he was planning on visiting, but he didn't need to. We had always been close, and anytime I got a chance to spend time with him, I was happy. It was strange to see him sleeping there with no sign of his wife anywhere, but there would be plenty of time the next day to get to the bottom of that. I just needed to get to sleep.

Turning around, I started away from the couch, trying to be as quiet as I could. Unfortunately, Brandon hadn't picked up many housekeeping skills after the age of sixteen and his shoes were tossed in the middle of the path to the hallway. The sound I made tripping over them woke him up, and his head popped up from the pillow, his expression nothing short of dazed and confused.

"Merry? Is that you?" he asked.

"Yep," I said.

"What's going on?" he asked, shifting to get up. "Are you okay?"

"Shh. Go back to sleep. I'm fine. I'm going to crash for a bit. See you in a few hours," I replied.

My brother nodded and curled further down into the couch, pulling the blanket up over his head. I was still curious about the whole situation as I made it into my bedroom, but I was also crashing from the adrenaline high of the win, and the alcohol was making my joints feel rubbery. Not even bothering to change out of my clothes, I toppled into bed.

I woke up the next morning to the uncomfortable reminders of why going to bed without bothering to go through any of the nighttime routines was not a good idea. Groaning, I rolled over and tried to pry open eyes glued together by old mascara while begrudging my unbrushed teeth. A quick glance at the clock beside my bed told me it was nine. That was plenty of sleep for me, and I knew once I managed to peel myself out of bed and get the remnants of the day before off, I'd feel much better.

As I sat up at the edge of the bed, pain shot through one temple and out the other, and my eyes felt like they were held in place by ill-fitting cotton balls. I closed my eyes and rubbed the lids with my fingertips. The sound of clattering and footsteps toward the front of my apartment startled me.

A shout and a few muttered profanities followed a crash from the direction of my kitchen, and I breathed a sigh of relief remembering that it was my brother. I went to the bathroom and climbed into a hot shower. The stinging water woke me up the rest of the way, and I felt back to normal by the time I got out, got dressed, and headed into the front of the apartment to find out what was going on. There was already a pot of coffee brewed, and I happily poured myself some. No matter how awake I felt, I would never turn down a cup of coffee in the morning.

Brandon was at the stove, rattling several pots and pans around. I watched him for a few seconds before speaking.

"What are you doing?" I asked.

"Making breakfast," he told me. "Omelets, home fries, cheese grits, and sausage."

There was definitely something bothering him. My brother loved to cook, but it was his coping mechanism. The more stressed and anxious he got, the more extreme his meals became. Considering there were only two of us and he was piling enough food on platters to serve a family of eight, this had to be serious.

"It's a really nice morning," I pointed out. "Want to eat on the patio?"

"Sure."

We each picked up platters and plates and carried them outside. I returned to the kitchen for coffee and juice, and he brought out glasses and silverware. When we were fully set up, I dished food out onto our plates as he poured juice. I waited for him to start the conversation, but he stayed quiet.

"Thanks for cooking," I said, trying to jump-start him into saying anything.

"No problem," he said. "So, you had that first race last night, right?"

I took a bite of the grits and nodded.

"Yeah, it was really good. The two riders came in first and third."

"That's pretty impressive," he said.

"Yeah, it was. It was really fun."

It was a completely inane conversation, but I wanted to keep him talking so eventually he would get to the point where he would tell me why he was at my apartment. We went back and forth for a little while talking about the race when he finally broke.

"Evelyn cheated on me," he said. "Apparently it's been going on for a few months. We're getting a divorce."

"I'm so sorry," I said. "I can't believe she did that."

"Neither can I," he agreed. "I couldn't even stand to look at her anymore. I just walked out after she told me with no plan and one duffle bag of old stuff. Sorry to crash your place, but it was the only place I could think of where I could just hang out and wouldn't be alone."

"Don't apologize. I'm glad you came here. This is where you should have come. And you can stay here for as long as you want. I have that spare room already set up so you don't have to crash on the couch. If you want, I can go back to your old place and get you some more stuff," I offered.

He shook his head. "I don't want to put you out. You already have enough going on with your new job and everything. You shouldn't have to be worried about me."

"You're the first thing I'm going to worry about," I told him. "My job is just a job. You are my big brother and you've always been there for me. No matter what kind of ridiculous crap I was going through, you were the one who made sure I got through it. Now it's my turn to take care of you."

He poked at his food with the tines of his fork and nodded, staring down at his lap so he didn't have to look at me. I could tell he was fighting hard not to cry, and I got up to give him a hug. Wrapping my arms around his shoulders, I rested my head on his. He gripped my arm and let out a long sigh.

"This fucking sucks," he said.

I laughed. "I think that about sums it up." Going back to my seat, I sat down and dove back into my breakfast. "All right. Here's the plan. I have to go into work for half a day, but when I get home, we'll figure things out. We'll get your stuff from the other house, figure out anything else you might need, order pizza, and watch terrible Japanese competition shows all night. Sound good?"

Brandon nodded. "Yeah, it does."

"Great."

I finished eating and went to finish getting ready for

work. It was shortly before eleven when I got to the complex and found it busier than I'd ever seen it. The energy was crazy with everyone still riding the high of the win. I didn't want to go inside the office building and sit behind the desk. The weather was so beautiful and sitting outside for breakfast had spoiled me for being inside for the entire day. Instead, I found a spot in the sunlight and sat down to work from my tablet. I started with making posts about the race the night before, then went back and checked on the other posts I'd been putting up to check for interaction.

It took another hour for me to respond to the various comments, do some retweeting, and schedule more posts for later in the week. The next day I would check in on the numbers of engagement and really see how everything was doing. That would be the real tell. If my plan was working, the numbers would show more hits, more followers, and more click-through. From those numbers I could determine what was working out well and what was falling flat with the audience. This was the part that was really fun for me. I enjoyed taking the pictures and coming up with the posts, but it was seeing the benefits that really excited me.

13

QUENTIN

Even though I told everybody they didn't have to be at work until after lunch, by the time I got to the complex around eleven-thirty, it was already busy. That didn't really surprise me. I was lucky to run a company with a team that really cared about what we were doing and wanted to put all they had into it. There wasn't a question in my mind about what this day would have been like if there wasn't such a good showing at the race the night before. Even if we had lost, the complex would still be busy and full of energy. Not the same excited energy—instead of an emotional high that was going to push them to keep going and stay on top, it would be a drive to redeem themselves and do better next time.

Their dedication was nothing short of inspiring, and it made me want to do better in everything I did for the company. Even when I felt like I gave my all and couldn't possibly push myself any harder, seeing them constantly reaching for that next goal made me look for any way I could improve and show them how much I appreciated their dedication.

That morning I parked in my usual spot, but instead of heading right into the office building, I started across the complex. I wanted to check in on Darren and Greg and see how they were feeling. Now that the initial adrenaline and thrill of the first and third place wins were gone, it was time to get back to business and start thinking strategically about the next race. All the other teams had now seen the modifications and improvements made to the bikes, and the new techniques the guys had come up with for the race itself. They would be better prepared the next time to counteract those efforts to try to secure the win for themselves. That meant we had to stay a step ahead and keep improving.

As I walked across the complex, I caught sight of Merry sitting in the sun with her tablet propped on her lap. She'd attached it to a small keyboard, and her fingers flew across the keys as she worked. The sun glittered on her hair where it was tied up away from her neck, revealing the delicate, graceful slope and her soft, smooth skin. At one point she closed her eyes and tilted her face up to get some of the light and warmth. It was a gesture I'd seen her do before when she was outside, but usually she followed it up with the satisfied, happy smile of someone who truly loved the sun and being outside to enjoy it. Only this time, she didn't get that smile. Instead, she let out a sigh that made her shoulders drop and looked back at the screen.

The expression on her face was tense. I couldn't really read the emotion, and that made me curious. I wanted to go up to her and ask her what was up but held myself back. She was obviously engrossed in her work, and I didn't want to bother her. If it did have something to do with work, I was sure she would make a point to tell me. We'd already discussed having regular meetings to talk about the social media campaign and how it was working out. I might not fully understand it, but that didn't mean I didn't want to be involved with it. This was my company, my legacy, and I didn't want anything happening without me being a part of it and having my say.

Moving on without disrupting her, I continued further into the complex. The practice track was empty, but I could hear voices coming from the shop. When I walked around to the back, I found the bay doors standing open and Darren and Dad inside. They stood in the middle of the floor surrounded by the pieces of a dismantled bike. I laughed.

"That bike got you to a first-place win in the first race of the season, and that's the thanks it gets?" I teased.

Darren looked up and smiled.

"I'm hoping it's going to get me to a bunch more first-place wins, but I have to make sure it stays in top shape for that to happen. I figured we could break it down and look at all the individual components again to see if there's anywhere else I could make improvements," he said.

"Haven't you been doing that for the last couple of months?" I asked, walking further into the workshop so I could survey how they had the elements of the bike laid out.

This was far from the first time I'd seen the two of them break apart a bike into each of its individual parts and scrutinize it. The same thing would happen several more times throughout the season as they made repairs, cleaned, and tuned the machine to keep it in its best condition until the very last race.

"In a way. A lot of the time I've been evaluating the whole bike or entire systems of it. Which is important, obviously, but doesn't give me the whole picture. It's been a while since I've actually broken it all the way down and looked at the individual parts. It performed really well last night, but I think it could be better. I want to tweak a few things and see what happens," he said.

"What are you looking at doing?" I asked.

I stood back and listened as my brother pointed out various parts of the bike and made comments about what he thought could be better about each. Though I was extremely familiar with the construction of the bike and how it worked, just knowing the mechanics wasn't comparable to his experience and knowledge of it. As the one who actually raced the bike, he had much more insight into how every component interacted with the others to perform in different situations. He was the one who could feel how the bike accelerated and responded to his commands when he was going through the turns or along the straightaways, how easily it could be used to pass other racers, and how stable it felt so he it was secure and safe in each stage of the race.

I wasn't completely unfamiliar with riding bikes. Of course, I spent my fair share of time on the backs of the machines. But I was never one to race them and didn't have the same level of connection to a bike that came from those experiences. Listening to him talk about what he felt and experienced during the race the night before and comparing that with the structural and functional knowledge I had of the bike let me give him suggestions for changes that could be made.

I spent the better part of the early afternoon there in the workshop with my brother and father, then headed over to the second workshop to check in with Greg. He was reviewing his own bike and making some modifications as well. It was interesting to see how differently he operated than Darren did. Both were skilled racers, but Greg was much more inward thinking. He liked to do things on his own, and while he was open to hearing suggestions and input from others, he rarely carried on brainstorming sessions with us.

Greg talked to me a bit about what he was doing with his bike and asked for my input on a few things he'd noticed during the race the night before. After another hour spent helping him, I realized I was completely exhausted. Breaking down everything after the bar the night before took longer than I expected it to, and even when I did finally get home, I didn't get much sleep. Despite being happy and tired, by the time I took a shower and dropped into bed, my brain wouldn't calm down. Thoughts of Merry had played in my head over and over again. Instead, I tossed and turned for a couple of hours before finally dropping off for a short stretch of sleep.

As much as I wanted to be a part of the post-race enthusiasm on the complex, I couldn't put in a whole day. My exhaustion would render me useless to anyone who needed anything from me. As I passed through the complex, I saw Merry still sitting in the same spot. It seemed like she hadn't gone anywhere all day, but I realized she must have moved at some point. There was now a large iced coffee sitting on the ground beside her, and on the other side, a piece of butcher paper spread across the grass held the remnants of a sandwich and a small paper cup that was probably once potato salad.

I recognized the food as coming from the small boxed lunch shop located up the road from the complex. She reached down and picked up the sandwich, taking a bite and setting it back down. My stomach tightened as she licked the tip of one of her fingers, and I tried to shove away the feeling, not wanting to acknowledge it. Her expression didn't look as distracted as before, which was a relief. She glanced up as I walked past, and I waved.

"Heading into the office?" she called.

I shook my head. "Calling it a day. I need some sleep."

She nodded. "Have a good one."

Those words took on a whole new meaning when I got home. I hoped I could just strip down to my boxers, stretch out across my bed, and have a solid nap. Maybe I'd get up feeling better and have a swim before dinner. But that didn't happen. Sleep continued to evade me when I lay down, and I found my mind wandering to images of Merry. The thought of her sitting there in the sun in her little sundress, her fingers in her mouth, made my body respond. I got hard just imagining her, and when my mind started conjuring new thoughts of her, images of her sexy body without the dress, and her mouth wrapped around my cock rather than her fingertip, I couldn't take the tension anymore.

I was at home. Alone. No one was going to judge me for what I was thinking. Closing my eyes and letting out a sigh, I slipped my hand down my shorts and wrapped it around my erection. Letting the thoughts of her dancing across my mind fuel me, I rubbed out a powerful orgasm and finally fell asleep.

14

MERRY

For the second day in a row, I woke up to the sound of banging around in my kitchen. My big brother and I were very close and always had been. We frequently visited each other and spent holidays staying either at his house or with our parents. I felt awful that he had been displaced from his home and was grateful that I had a place he could come to and lick his wounds.

I couldn't even imagine what he was going through. He and Evelyn had been married for five years and were together for a long time before that. He wasn't just dealing with knowing his wife had betrayed him and broken his heart and his trust. He was also having to wrap his head around a completely different life moving forward.

Right now, what we had to think about was how he was going to do that. I'd already given him the room and told him he could have it for as long as he needed, no rent required. It didn't seem right to ask him to pay rent right now. Not only was his career totally up in the air, but I had been going right along in the apartment by myself without a problem. Unless he started attempting to drown his sorrows in four-hour showers every day, I didn't need the money to pay for the apartment. He planned on contributing by buying groceries, and that was plenty for me.

Dressed and ready for work, I walked out to the kitchen and poured my customary cup of coffee. Brandon stood at the stove flipping pancakes on a griddle. I made a mental note to check out the fitness room in the apartment complex. If he was going to continue to express his emotions through fat and carbs, I was going to need to get out ahead of it fast. I wasn't about to turn down any of the food he cooked, but there needed to be a bit of balance.

"So, I was thinking," I said after the first few sips of coffee gave my brain a caffeine boost. I was still learning to be functional enough to carry on a conversation first thing in the morning. "You were saying you didn't want to keep going at the firm."

"Not happening," he said. "Jim and Karen are perfectly nice, and I feel bad leaving them in a lurch, but I can't stroll in there like nothing happened knowing they are getting every detail of the divorce from Evelyn's perspective. Not to mention if she came in with him, I might not be able to control what I do."

"And that's totally understandable. So, that means we start looking for a new position for you. How is your resume?" I asked.

"Not updated. I didn't really think I was ever going to have to look for another job," he admitted. "I figured that was going to be my career right up until I retired. Jim even talked about Evelyn and me taking over when he was ready to retire in a few years."

"Okay. Then there's a place to start. Today while I'm at

the office, start putting together your resume. We'll take it from there," I told him.

He agreed and brought over the platter of pancakes. As we ate, I thought about his future and how much I wished I could do something more to help him. I wished I could bring him along with me so he could work for Freeman. The family was great, the rest of the team was amazing, and I knew he would fit right in. But I hadn't been working there long enough to ask them to hire my brother. That seemed like I was overreaching my place in the company. Besides, with that type of organization, I was sure they probably had an established accountant already.

When we were finished with breakfast, I gathered everything I needed for work, then stopped by to see him again.

"You already have your extra key. I'm going to talk to the landlord at lunch and let her know you're staying here. I'll get you added to the lease," I told him.

"You don't need to go out of your way to do that," he said. "I'm going to get out of your hair soon."

"You're not in my hair, and it's not going out of my way. You'll stay here. It's good to have you around, and you don't need to be dealing with trying to find your own place and everything while all this is going on. Stick around until everything is more settled and you're on your feet again. Besides, getting you on the lease is just so she doesn't freak out if she's in the complex and sees some guy on the patio. I don't want her to think I'd been invaded or anything," I said.

He laughed. The sound wasn't completely full like I was used to, but it was something. I would take any little flashes of him that showed he was gradually climbing out of the gloom. It would take time. This wasn't something he was just going to get over in the snap of his fingers. It didn't matter what she'd done and how much she'd hurt him. My brother loved Evelyn, and it was going to hurt for a long time. But I was going to be there for him in every way I could, and eventually he would have life in his control again.

"I'm going to go by the house today and get some stuff," he told me.

"You're sure you don't want to wait so I can go with you?" I asked.

He shook his head. "I'll be fine. She's going to be at work, so I won't run into her. It will be easier for me to just go in, get it done, and have it over with."

"Well, if you change your mind, call me. I can meet you there after work."

"I will."

I hugged him and left, knowing that was going to be much harder for Brandon than he was letting on. He wasn't just going back to the house he shared with her to get clothes and personal belongings. He was facing off against the life he'd left behind and extracting himself from it piece by piece. That was going to be tough, and I started to think of ways I could make him feel better when I got home. A round of some of the board games we used to play when we were younger might be in order.

I was at my desk a couple of hours later going over some of the early reports when Quentin leaned in through the open door. He rapped his knuckles on the doorframe and smiled at me when I looked up at him.

"How's it going, Stats?" he asked.

I stared at him for a few silent seconds. There was something different about him. He'd been more pleasant toward me the last few times we'd interacted, but not like this. And what was that "stats" business? I didn't know if he had just given me a nickname or if that word meant something else to him.

"It's going fine," I finally answered. "Just checking the hashtags to see which have been the most effective ones. I'll keep tracing them for a few days and then decide which ones to swap out with different ones that may be more appealing. All part of the process."

He nodded, his smile seeming stuck across his face and his eyes just a little too wide.

"You looked a little off yesterday, like you were angry or upset about something. Is everything okay?" he asked.

This took me aback. Not only did I not realize I'd been showing any kind of signs of what might be going through my head, but I was surprised he'd noticed it. I didn't think my mood was something that would even register to Quentin in the normal course of a day, much less stick with him enough to have him ask me about it. Especially as awkwardly as he was.

"Um, yeah. Family stuff," I told him. "My brother is going through a tough time, and I'm trying to help him out."

I didn't want to go into a bunch of detail and make it uncomfortable, but I figured that was vague enough to be appropriate for the work environment. Quentin looked at me for another silent stretch, like he was waiting for more, then realized I wasn't going to tell him anything else. He grinned a little wider and patted his hand against the doorframe like he was telling a driver to go.

"Well, we like to think of everybody around here as a big family, so if you need something, just give me a holler."

He said it like he didn't sound for all the world like an

after-school special and walked away. I watched him until long after I couldn't hear his footsteps going down the hall anymore. The thought flickered through my mind wondering if this could possibly be the same man I met on my first day, or if he'd somehow gotten replaced by an awkwardly smiley clone.

15

QUENTIN

With the first race done and won, it left us fully in the thick of the season. Even with the high of doing well, the pressure around the complex was elevated. It might even be higher because of the win. Performing so well meant we had a precedent we had to uphold. We were at the top, which meant the only way Darren had to go was down. Greg's performance could only improve slightly but getting us up to the first two places would be extremely impressive. We couldn't get complacent and just expect to keep doing well. The other teams weren't sitting on their laurels, so we couldn't, either.

Dad had been more involved since the race than he had been in months, spending all day in the workshops with the mechanics. Darren could do a lot of the work on his own bike, but when it came to the most intricate of changes and repairs, as well as the basic maintenance that kept the machines in top shape, we relied on a team of skilled mechanics. They had been working with us for years, which I always thought gave us an advantage over teams that had frequent turnover in their crews.

We, on the other hand, had the same mechanics we'd been using for more than a decade. They knew all of us well, and we knew them just as well. Understanding each other translated to a better understanding of the work that needed to be done. Because they were familiar with how Darren rode, they could recommend alterations to the bike that would enhance his skills while compensating for weaknesses. For those on the outside of the racing industry, it seemed like a massive amount of work and effort just to try to squeeze a fraction of a second more speed out of the bike. But for those in the race, that fraction of a second could make all the difference.

I expected to find Darren in the workshop working with the mechanics, but instead, it was only Dad.

"Where's Darren?" I asked. "With Greg?"

Dad shook his head. "No. Greg spent the morning making some tweaks with the guys, and now he's running some tests rides on the track. Darren is off with Victor."

I laughed. "Ah. All right, you guys keep up the good work. I'll talk to you later."

Darren being with Victor meant he had returned to his single-minded mission to trim off a few pounds. The lighter the rider, the faster the bike, and he had it in his head he could shave off some weight and be an even better competitor.

Next, I made my way into the main office building. Immediately, I smelled cinnamon and headed to the employee kitchen. Just as I expected, I found Mom in there, surrounded by baked goods. She was leaned over at the oven pulling out a fresh batch of cinnamon rolls, which she placed on a cooling rack on the counter beside a huge bowl of cream cheese frosting. Baking up a storm was how Mom always handled stress.

The kitchen was also where I found Merry. She and Glenda were standing over a plate of brownies, and I salivated as Merry broke off a piece of one and placed it between her full lips, licking the fudgy remnants from her fingers when she was finished.

"It's funny. Minnie was just saying she does all this baking when she's feeling stressed out or worried about something. That's exactly what's going on with my brother. He's at my house cooking all the time because he's upset about the divorce and having to leave his job," Merry said.

"So, you have it coming at you from all directions," Glenda laughed.

"You're right about that. After eating everything he's been making for me, I thought coming to work was going to be my safe space. But now we've got Minnie Stewart over here making the most delicious goodies in the world."

"I'm sorry to hear about your brother, though. That's really rough," Glenda told her.

Merry nodded. "The divorce is really sad, and I know he's upset about it, but she cheated, so that is what it is. His job is what's really getting to me. He worked so hard to get where he was and had so many hopes for the future. It's terrible because he's really good at his job. Working with his in-laws was great for him. He was being groomed to take over the company one day, and everything seemed set. Until his floosy of a wife decided to blow that all to hell, and now he has no wife, no house, and no job," Merry said.

I felt guilty about eavesdropping, but this explained why she looked upset when she was sitting outside working, and it gave me a little more information.

"That's awful," Glenda commiserated. "What is it that he does?"

"He's an accountant," Merry said, breaking off another piece of brownie and bringing it to her lips.

That was the magic word. I sidled up to the counter and leaned in close.

"We're looking for a new accountant. Our guy is about to retire. Probably a good thing. He's like a hundred," I said. Merry's eyes snapped to me, wide with shock, and she swallowed her bite in a deliberate movement. I realized that approach wasn't the best. "Sorry. I overheard you talking, and you mentioned your brother's an accountant. I was just thinking we needed to look for a new accountant to replace Artie, so it jumped out at me. But, really. Your brother needs a job, we need a numbers guy. Tell him to talk to my mom, and we can see if he's a good fit."

I walked away quickly, not even giving Merry the chance to respond. I crossed the kitchen right to the pan of cinnamon rolls Mom was dousing in cream cheese frosting. She protested as I reached in and grabbed one of the rolls. The still incredibly hot pastry sizzled on my fingertips and the melting frosting was sticky. Mom's cinnamon rolls were worth the inconvenience. That and I needed anything available to get me out of the conversation with Merry.

Getting a cup of coffee, I left the kitchen and hurried to my office where I could close the door and be alone with all my disquieting thoughts. And there were plenty of them. It felt weird being so invested in helping her and her brother. I could tell how worried she was and how much she wanted to help him figure his life out, and as soon as she mentioned the accountant, the offer just popped out of my mouth. I didn't even get a chance to think it all the way through before I said it and had her looking at me like I was a total maniac.

But it wasn't just that. I could barely even look her in

the eye. I needed to snatch my cinnamon bun and run as fast as I could because it was too awkward to stand there and look at her with the memories of jerking off to fantasies of her in my mind still so fresh. It was the hardest I'd come in a long time thinking about all the things I wanted to do to her.

As much as I enjoyed it and it released the tension I was feeling, it put me in a weird place I wasn't familiar with. With Merry, even without her knowing, I felt like I was crossing lines with her left and right.

Offering to have Mom interview her brother wasn't about my attraction to her, though. I told myself that a dozen times as I ate the cinnamon roll and shot Artie a quick email to have him come in for a meeting. That offer was purely about business and what was going to be beneficial for everybody. We really did need the help. Artie had been working for Freeman Racing for even longer than the mechanics. Most of them had come along no more than fifteen years ago. Artie was the accountant around here even when Dad owned Freeman Racing and it was just a tiny operation. Nothing like what I'd built it into.

Artie had started talking about retiring two years before but had never gotten around to it. He was too committed to the company, and we never had anyone lined up to take his place. Of everyone working at the complex, he definitely ranked among the hardest working, and he deserved to spend the rest of his life in a recliner somewhere. I looked forward to being able to tell him he could feel good about retiring and enjoying his golden years.

16

MERRY

"What's the best breakfast to eat before an important interview?" I asked when Brandon came into the kitchen the next morning.

He stared at me through sleepy eyes, apparently shocked to find me awake before him and already brewing the pot of coffee that he had gotten used to making. I probably should have thought about that before I did it. For anyone else, brewing a pot of coffee wouldn't be that big of a deal. It was just stuffing the carafe into place and hitting a couple of buttons. But for my brother, it was the routine that really mattered. He was nothing if not a creature of habit. Those habits were what kept him feeling like he had some control in his life, especially now. He had to change the ones he already had and find new habits, but even in the few days he'd been living with me again, he'd latched onto certain ones.

Getting him out of the apartment and back to work would be just what Brandon needed to start feeling normal again.

"Um. French toast?" he asked.

"Is there any scientific or anecdotal merit to that, or are you just pulling out the first thing you thought of?" I asked.

"First thing I thought of. I don't think there is an official breakfast for the morning of an interview you never thought you were going to have to have after walking away from the career you spent your adult life building because your wife had an affair and you're getting a divorce," he said flatly.

"You sure do know how to take the zip out of a morning with your sparkling attitude and incredibly long sentences," I told him.

He shrugged and went about gathering the ingredients for French toast. It was a favorite breakfast of ours growing up. Our mother would make it for us on special occasions like birthdays and holidays.

"So, you remember, Quentin is the owner of the company. He took over for his father, Gus, when the older Freeman retired years ago. At least, Gus is supposed to be retired. He actually spends most of his time at the complex, anyway. His wife, Minnie, is the one who will interview you. She handles the hiring. She's really sweet, and she bakes when she is feeling stressed, so that should give you something to talk about."

"Yes, because nothing says I'm a responsible and reliable professional you should hire to manage the finances of your company quite like discussing mental instability and suffocating stress," Brandon pointed out.

"Just keep it in your pocket unless the topic comes up for some reason," I said.

As he made breakfast, I went to his room to raid the clothes he'd gotten from his old house. Like I expected, most of them were the stuffy clothes he wore to work every day at the firm. Those weren't going to fit in at the complex. Though I was sure he would have been just fine if he did show up in a suit and want to work that way, I was getting used to the Freeman family and had a feeling they would be more comfortable with him in a more casual outfit. Still professional and put together, but not so stark. I chose a pair of slacks and a polo shirt. I laid them out on his bed and went back into the kitchen to put together a fruit salad to have alongside the French toast.

"Darren is the youngest brother. He's the racer. Greg is their other rider who just started racing with them, but he isn't one of the brothers."

"How many brothers did you say there are?" Brandon asked.

"Four. Vince and Nick aren't technically part of the company, but they're around sometimes for specific things. They come to races and events," I told him.

I continued the rundown on the family, the complex, and everything I'd learned about the company as he got dressed and we drove to the complex. It wasn't until we got there that I realized I hadn't even asked him if he was interested in the position. Instead, I came home full of excitement and informed him he had an appointment in the morning to be interviewed for the accountant position. I didn't even really remember his reaction. Maybe I should have waited to see how he felt about it before all but dragging him to the complex and throwing him through the window of Minnie's office to make sure he got there. At the same time, Brandon wasn't great at change and might be hesitant to jump in if I didn't give him that push. I knew this was the perfect position for him, and it would mean we would get to work together, which we'd never done before.

We got to the complex, and I brought him directly to Minnie's office. The door was closed, so I led him to a chair outside and pushed his shoulders down to seat him.

"All right. Here we are. She should be out any minute. She knows you're coming. I told her I'd bring you here first thing in the morning when we talked yesterday. Remember, her name is Minnie. Do well," I said.

"Don't think this means you get to be the older sibling forever, now," he said. "Eventually I'm going to figure myself out again, and I'm going to take that back. But Mom and Dad would be amused."

He was right. They would think it was hilarious the little girl who followed Brandon around and had said his name as her first word would be taking care of him now.

I was reluctant to leave him alone there in the chair. I wanted to just hover there and wait for Minnie to come and take him in for the interview, then wait until he came out to learn the news. But I forced myself to walk away. This wasn't the first day of kindergarten, and I wasn't dropping my little boy off for the first time. He was a grown man going to what was not his first job interview, and he would survive just fine.

Once in my office, I did my best to distract myself with work. The whiteboard had been reconfigured with new hashtags and some were erased, so I stood and examined them for a while, adding a few, making notes in color-coded ink next to others. When that ran out of usefulness, I went back to my desk and sat there going over posts, working on the new blog I was putting together for the company, and engaging with a few fans who were online. All the while I kept one ear to the door, waiting to hear Brandon come to tell me how it went.

Finally, I heard footsteps and I jumped up, but it was Quentin. I realized I felt a little burst of happiness in my chest when I saw it was him and told myself to knock it off. Those weren't thoughts I should be having about my boss.

"Good to see you, too," he laughed.

I shook my head and settled back into my chair.

"I thought you were my brother coming to tell me how his interview went," I said.

"Oh, is he here today?" Quentin asked.

"Yes. He's in with your mother now. Thank you, by the way, for the recommendation. I really appreciate it. And so does he."

"Not a problem. If it's a good fit, it's really helping both of us out. Besides, like I said, I try to keep the company feeling like a family affair. We like how you're doing and feel like you fit in with that, so bringing him aboard just makes sense," Quentin said.

I was floored by the declaration. I thought I was doing well, and the results from fan engagement were showing it, but Quentin going out of his way to say that was unexpected. But I didn't get much of a chance to think it through because suddenly Brandon was standing there behind Quentin. I jumped up again, and Quentin turned around, stepping out of the way to let my brother inside. Brandon turned to him and extended a hand.

"Brandon Holster," he said. "You must be Quentin Freeman."

Quentin took his hand.

"Yes. You're Merry's brother? The accountant?" he asked.

"Yes. I can't thank you enough for the opportunity."

"Absolutely. Glad to do it," Quentin said. "How did the interview go?"

"Yeah, Brandon. How did it go?" I asked.

He turned slowly, then flashed me a grin, and I squealed with excitement. Running around from behind the desk, I gave him a hug.

"Congratulations!" I said. "That's amazing. I'm so happy for you."

"I am, too," he said.

"We have to celebrate. Bar tonight. You and me. Olivia. Quentin, if you want to come. Invite some of the guys," I said.

"That sounds great," Brandon said. "I'll make some calls."

"Great. Quentin?" I asked.

"I might be able to do that. A buddy of mine is coming back into town tonight, so if I make it, he'll be coming with me," he answered.

I nodded, not really paying attention to anything beyond him saying he might come.

17

QUENTIN

All day I had been excited to finish up work and get home. I'd been eagerly anticipating Cole getting back in town for so long, and he'd finally landed the day before. I offered to pick him up at the airport, but his flight didn't land until the middle of the night and he said he didn't want to inconvenience me like that. As a welcome-home surprise, I hired a town car, so a chauffeur was waiting for him at the luggage claim, white gloves and holding a sign with his name on it and everything. It was the kind of thing that would make him laugh, and I wish I was there to see his reaction. Cole was definitely not a fancy-car-and-personal-driver type of guy. He wouldn't really care what kind of vehicle pulled up at the curb in front of him as long as it had four functioning tires and got him home in one piece.

Having the elegant, expensive car waiting for him was the kind of ribbing he and I did to each other all the time. We'd been friends most of our lives, since well before I'd built up the company and racked up the millions in my bank account. Knowing me before my success meant he got to make fun of me for becoming one of those rich guys who didn't know how to do anything for himself. He knew that wasn't the case, but it meant I could in turn make fun of him for being one of the common class or make him uncomfortable by putting him in fussy situations like the hired car. It had been a long time since we'd seen each other, so it felt good to get back to the usual routine.

I was fully expecting some kind of joke in return that night, and I looked forward to catching up with him. Cole's situation was one of the reasons I felt so much compassion toward Merry's brother and wanted to do anything I could to help him. Like Brandon, Cole had recently gone through a divorce. It was pretty brutal, and by the time it was over, he was a shell of his former self. I tried everything I could think of to help him pull through and get back to the person he used to be, but that was something he had to do on his own. It was only a few weeks after the divorce was finalized when he came to me and said he was going to Tibet for six months.

Of course, the first thing I did was ask him why on Earth he would do something like that. He told me it was to get himself back. Those were his exact words. I promptly joked I thought his ex-wife got him in the divorce just like she got everything else. In retrospect, that probably wasn't the best thing for me to say. But he was decent enough to force a laugh, say that wasn't too far from the truth, and admit he felt like he just needed some time away from his normal life to figure out who he was again. He and his wife were high school sweethearts, and it was easy to see he didn't really know who he was as a person without her alongside him.

As soon as I opened my door and saw him standing on the porch, though, I could see he was back. There was a sparkle in his eyes that hadn't been there in a long time, even well before they filed for divorce. He was skinnier, but he looked happier and more at peace. His face broke out in a huge grin, and he reached out to pull me in a hug, pounding me on the back a few times.

"I missed you," I told him. "It's so good to see you man."

"It's so good to see you, too," he told me. "Nice trick with the driver last night. I told him to charge a five-hundred-dollar tip to whatever payment method you used."

I laughed.

"Fair enough. Come on in. Are you hungry?" I asked.

He followed me inside and let out an exasperated sound.

"Everybody is asking me if I'm hungry," he said. "I went to see my mom this morning, and the first thing she said was 'are you hungry?' Then I stopped by my sister's house, and she asked if I was hungry. Is that some sort of new conventional greeting that's spread around the country and I missed it while I was gone?"

"No, it's just your skinny ass looks like it needs a burger or two," I told him.

"Yeah, probably," he said. "Turns out Tibet is not all that big on fast-food restaurants. Not a whole lot of pizza joints, either."

I laughed again. "Good to know you did thorough research before going on your spirit quest."

He sat down on one of the tall stools at my kitchen island, and I took out a plate of cheese and sausage I liked to keep in the refrigerator to snack on. Adding a box of crackers, I leaned on the other side of the counter and we dug in.

"So, what are we doing tonight?" he asked after we spent a while catching up and swapping stories about the six months we'd been apart.

"Actually, I did have an idea. How do you feel about going to a bar for a couple of drinks?" I asked.

"Sounds good. Are you meeting the crew up there?"

"Not exactly," I told him. "Actually, we were invited by a new employee. Her brother just got hired in to, so she wanted to celebrate. She's bringing a couple of people, and I told her we might stop by. But we don't have to if it doesn't sound like something you want to do."

"No, that sounds like fun. It doesn't really sound like something you would do, though," he pointed out.

"What do you mean?" I asked.

"I don't really think of you as the type to go out drinking with your employees unless it's after a race," he said. "Who is this girl?"

"Her name is Merry. She's the social media consultant," I explained.

Cole laughed so hard I thought he might choke on the chunk of cheese he'd just put in his mouth.

"Social media consultant?" he asked. "You seriously hired a social media consultant? Who the hell are you, and what did you do with my best friend while I was up in the mountains scared out of my mind a yeti was going to eat me?"

"Mom hired her," I said, frowning.

"Well, that sounds more like it. Minnie is definitely the type to try to keep things up-to-date."

"Are you trying to say something?" I asked.

"That you're an old man stuffed into a 40-year-old body? Yes, that's exactly what I'm trying to say," he teased.

"Very funny. I'm on the cutting-edge now. You can check all the platforms for yourself. The company is on all of them, and they are actually kept current. Thanks to Merry," I told him.

Cole instantly called my bluff and pulled out his phone to start scanning through the various postings. His eyes widened, and then he turned the phone so I can look at the screen. There was an image of Merry at the race with Mom, and he pointed at it.

"Is that her?" he asked.

"Yes," I said. "That's at the first race of the season."

"Now I can see why you wanted a social media consultant," he muttered.

"It's not like that," I told him. "She's my employee. Just like you said. The only reason I agreed to go out tonight is it was I thought you would like to have some fun after getting home and she wanted to celebrate her brother getting the job. It seemed rude if I turned her down."

"All right. If that's what you're going to go with, I will join right in with the delusion. Let's go," he said.

The bar was loud and crowded as usual. I wasn't used to being there when we weren't blowing off steam after a long week or celebrating a win. It felt a little awkward walking in and realizing I didn't have the entire company there. It was just about the small group socializing. But I decided not to think about it. I was too happy that Cole was back and just wanted to enjoy it. And if I let myself be honest for a moment, I was looking forward to spending some time with Merry outside of work.

We eventually found the rest of the group at a large booth in the back corner. I introduced everybody and asked if anybody needed a drink. They all agreed, and I made my way toward the bar. I was already feeling more at ease now that we had settled in. I like Brandon and thought he would be a good addition to the team just like his sister was.

Ordering a round of drinks, I added an assortment of food and made my way back to the table. Three waitresses showed up just a few moments later with pint glasses and pitchers of beer, then the baskets of food and a stack of plates. We all dove in, and very quickly the night turned into something a college-aged me would be very proud of.

"Who's ready for a game of darts?" Merry's friend Olivia asked.

"You're on," Brandon said, and they made their way over to the dartboard.

The rest of us followed suit and set up a miniature tournament. It was the first time Merry and I were in close enough proximity to actually speak directly to each other, and I leaned down slightly to her.

"You're not some sort of dart hustler, are you?" I asked.

She looked up at me and laughed.

"I'm not a dart anything," she said. "Be prepared to be dazzled by my exceptional lack of skill."

She grabbed a handful of darts and stepped out for her turn. Her evaluation of herself was not an understatement. She completely missed the board twice, and the one time she hit it was on the very edge. She twirled around, arms up in the air as if she had just accomplished something amazing, and Olivia laughed, applauding her enthusiastically.

"That was exceptionally terrible," I told her when she came back to my side. "But, if you were a hustler, that would be how you would start. So, I still have my eye on you."

I tried to ignore the blush that crept up her neck at my words and just how tight my pants had started to feel.

The rest of the game proved she definitely wasn't hustling, and by the end of it, we were all laughing and taking back our third round of beer. Cole pointed across the bar to the beer pong table that had been occupied by actual college-age people throughout the entire night. It was suddenly vacant, and we scooted over to claim it. Waitresses came over with more beer to fill the cups, and we positioned ourselves on either end of the table, guys on one side, girls on the other. No one else had ventured out to join us that night, so the teams ended up lopsided: Brandon, Cole, and me on one side, and Olivia and Merry on the other.

"I'll be referee," Brandon offered. "That way it'll be even."

"You don't have to do that," Merry said.

"I really should, though. You see, I just got this new job, and I hear my new boss is a real hard-ass," he said.

"I don't know where you heard that," Merry said, mocking innocence and I had to laugh.

We played a couple of rounds before Merry and I both headed toward the bathroom. On the way out, I ended up in a crush of people and suddenly got pushed. I didn't realize she was in front of me until I rammed into her and she turned around to look at me. I reached out to wrap my arms around her and stop us both from falling. The heat of her body was new and exciting, and I didn't let her go. Instead, I pulled her up closer and walked with her down to the end of the hall where there wasn't anyone else.

The next thing I knew, we were kissing. I had her pressed to the wall, her body still close to mine, and my hands around her waist. She looped her arms around my neck and leaned into the kiss, opening her mouth to the guiding pressure of my tongue until it tangled with hers. I never wanted to stop kissing her. But a few seconds later, I heard a familiar voice.

"Quentin?"

I looked up and saw Cole standing a few feet away in the hallway. Merry and I quickly disentangled ourselves, and she scurried away back toward the table.

"Sorry about that," he said. "I didn't mean to interrupt."

"It's fine. You ready to go?" I asked.

Cole had already called a rideshare, and it was waiting for us outside. The entire drive home all I could think about was Merry's sweet mouth and hot body pressed up against me and wondered if maybe this was the upheaval I'd been anticipating.

18

MERRY

I seriously did not want to open my eyes. In those first couple of moments of not being asleep anymore, but not yet being all the way awake, I could already feel the thudding reminder of the fun I'd had the night before. Eventually, I was going to have to open my eyes to the cruelty of light and awareness, and it was all going to come crashing down onto me.

Which was going to suck.

I lay there in bed with my pillow over my head and the blankets pulled up over my shoulders for as long as I possibly could. Finally, I didn't have any choice but to get up, and the full hangover hit me.

And it definitely sucked.

I dragged myself to the bathroom and took a shower, standing under the hot water with the hopes it would do... something. It accomplished little but made me feel less woozy, and I got out, dressed in a pair of yoga pants and a stretchy tank top and headed for the kitchen. The smell of coffee was all the encouragement I needed. There was no work that day, and I intended on doing nothing but setting myself up with a constant drip of the strongest coffee my maker could produce, eating salty fried food, and stretching out on the couch to pray to the gods of reality TV that I'd make it through.

This wasn't my first hangover, but I hadn't had enough in my life to not be a complete sissy when it came to them. I got to the kitchen and found Brandon standing by the coffee maker, the carafe in his hand. Getting my mug from the cabinet, I reached for the pot, but he pulled it away.

"Morning, sunshine," he said. "Sleep well?"

"Give me the coffee, Brandon," I said. "Hand it over slowly and no one gets hurt."

He grinned like an asshole and pulled the pot further away again.

"You know I didn't think you had it in you," he said.

"What?" I asked in confusion.

"Having the hots for your boss." That stopped me. I stared at him, my head tilting to the side.

"What are you talking about?" I asked.

"You totally have the hots for your boss," he said again. "You know, I never really pegged you for that kind of girl. Teacher's pet, maybe. But not a desk bunny."

"First, gross. Second, and I repeat with augmentation, what the hell are you talking about?" I asked.

He finally put down his guard enough for me to grab the pot of coffee from him and pour myself a cup. I didn't even bother adding my usual cream and sugar and just downed half of it in one burning, ill-advised gulp.

"You don't remember making out with him last night?" Brandon asked.

I choked and stared at him, wiping the droplets of coffee away from my bottom lip.

"Excuse me?" I asked.

Brandon laughed disbelievingly and took back the coffeepot for his own cup.

"Seriously?" he asked. "You really don't remember? How much did you drink?"

"Well, my team wasn't very good at beer pong," I said.

He laughed again. "Sure. That's the excuse that we'll go with."

"What happened last night?" I asked. "All I remember is being there with you guys and meeting Quentin's friend Cole. I know we played darts and beer pong. But all of that is kind of fuzzy. What else happened?"

"You mean before or after Cole caught you two making out in the hallway by the bathroom?" Brandon asked

"Oh, no," I said. "Are you serious? Did that actually happen, or are you just trying it to get a rise out of me?"

I knew the answer. There was no other reason he would be taunting me for having the hots for my boss. I obviously hadn't told him about any of the feelings I thought I might be having toward Quentin, and I hadn't said or done anything to even suggest it as far as I knew.

"I didn't see it for myself, but you sure came running back fast, and when Cole came back in because he forgot his wallet and you were back in the bathroom with Olivia, he had a story to tell," Brandon said.

I groaned, covering my face with my hands. It wasn't enough. I wanted to bury my head in some sand somewhere and not come out for a while. But since there was no sand around anywhere, I would have to settle for the couch. Setting my mug down on the counter with a thud, I went into the living room and toppled over face-first onto the cushions.

"Oh, no. I can't believe I did that. How could I do that?" I lamented into the pillows.

"It's all right," Brandon said.

I felt him come to the side of the couch and sit down on the edge of the cushions. He patted my back.

"No, it's not," I said, shaking my head but not lifting it. "I made out with my boss in the back of a grimy bar."

"It's not that grimy of a bar," he said.

"Does that make a difference about me making out with him?" I asked.

"Well, no. I was just trying to make you feel better."

"It didn't work. What the fuck am I going to do?" I asked, the sudden realization that I might have just ruined my career popping up in my mind.

"Relax, I'm sure it'll be fine. Chalk it up to a drunken mistake and get over it. If you don't make a big deal over it, I bet he won't either," Brandon said.

I nodded and then buried my face back in the cushions.

Brandon laughed and patted me on the back.

"You made fun of me while I was hungover," I said, my voice muffled.

"I know. I'm your big brother, it's my job. But I'm sorry. How about some breakfast?" he asked.

Flopping over onto my side and dragging in a breath, I nodded.

"Something greasy," I said.

Brandon smiled, and for a moment I saw my carefree big brother again. I was hoping to see more of him, to really have my brother all the way back soon. He was always going to have some of the quirks—they were just part of him—but I'd like to see him relax some. Working at Freeman could really help that. A less intense work environment could help him feel more comfortable and put him in a better mindset.

He headed into the kitchen and started cooking as I

reached for the remote. Turning on the TV, I found it wasn't actually morning anymore. I'd managed to sleep my way into the afternoon, and I didn't feel an ounce bad about it. In fact, I was going to sleep more if I got the chance.

I'd watched almost a full episode of a delightfully trashy live court show when my brother came back out of the kitchen with a tray heaping with food and a bottle of pain reliever. That marked the beginning of my day not leaving the couch except to go to the bathroom.

By the time Brandon was cooking dinner, I felt better enough to realized I hadn't checked in on Olivia yet. According to my brother, she was still at the bar when he'd poured me into the back of a car and brought me home. Since I hadn't gotten even so much as a text from her, I was starting to worry. Fortunately, the worry was for nothing. She answered in a groggy voice, and I knew she was dealing with the same head full of lead and cotton I was.

"You doing okay?" I asked.

"If by okay you mean alive, then yes," she said.

"I'll take it. Brandon tells me you stayed at the bar after we left."

"Do you remember the cute bartender?"

"Vaguely. I mean, I remember there *was* a bartender. And that you talked to him a lot. So, yeah, I guess," I said.

"Well, we just kept flirting and I ended up closing down the place with him," she told me.

"Way to go. I'm proud of you, Liv," I said.

"I'm proud of you, too. Kissing the sexy boss in the dark bar. More my style, but I like it."

"And there it is," I groaned. "I was really hoping somehow that had missed you."

"How could it miss me?" she asked. "You dragged me into the bathroom after he left and told me about it."

"I did?" I asked, rubbing my forehead. "Well, at least I was gossiping about myself and you aren't just teasing me like Brandon."

"You have to admit, it's pretty funny," Olivia said.

"No, I don't. Because it's not."

"I think it is," she said with a giggle.

"I don't even remember it. And I'm glad you all find it so amusing, but I'm actually worried I'm going to lose my job because of it," I told her.

"Why?"

"It's not exactly what he hired me for," I pointed out.

We chatted for a bit longer before the pain rushed back into my head, and I got off the phone. While Brandon and I ate, I thought about how I was going to handle going back to work. This wasn't something I could just pretend didn't happen like Brandon suggested. Even if he was like me and woke up not realizing what had happened, chances were Quentin had heard the news from Cole. I needed to be prepared to handle this head-on. By the time I crawled into bed that night, I'd worked out a pretty solid conversation to have with Quentin on Monday morning in hopes he wouldn't fire me for breaking some sort of fraternizing rule.

19

QUENTIN

Sunday was usually the day I had my brothers and parents over for family night. I normally looked forward all week long to hanging out with them around the fire and catching up. Even though I worked with most of them and talked with Vince and Nick on almost a daily basis, it was still good to just be able to get together and relax every week. But I just couldn't do it today. It was already early afternoon by the time I managed to pry my eyes open and fight through the headache searing through to the back of my brain. Thankful for the family group text we maintained, I jotted out a quick message to cancel the usual gathering, saying I needed a breather before we started to gear up for the race on Wednesday.

I knew they would understand. We'd already been pushing so hard, and the days leading up to the race would be even more intense. We'd been putting in more hours, and it would be stressful and tiring, so all of us having a day to just kick back and relax made sense. In reality, I needed to talk to Cole. Though my memory of the night before was fuzzy when I first got up, it didn't take long for me to remember being in that hallway. I could still feel Merry's body against mine and taste her kiss.

"Tell me something," I said when he came over that afternoon and we were floating around the pool. "What happened?"

"I thought I already told you all this. You said you were going to the bathroom, and you were gone for way too long and I came to make sure you hadn't gotten sick and passed out or anything, and I found you and your social media guru attempting to swallow each other whole against the wall," Cole told me.

"I meant before that. When Merry first started working for the company, I didn't exactly want her around. I thought it was ridiculous that Mom even thought we needed a social media consultant, and she aggravated the hell out of me. The first time I met her, I couldn't help but snap at her. How did I get from there to here?"

"Uhh, because she's crazy hot?" he said.

"Well yes, but I'm not a damn caveman and can usually control my baser impulses. Especially around my damn employees," I said.

Cole just smiled at me. "I think you've liked her from the get-go and that's why she annoyed you. Your response to the attraction was to push her away because you're afraid to let anyone get close to you again."

I blinked a few times, processing what he said.

"Wow. Being in the mountains with the monks really did clear your mind, didn't it?" I asked flatly.

"Seriously," Cole said. "Think about it. You don't have the greatest track record with relationships. And you've managed to keep yourself totally disjointed from anything having to do with a real connection to a woman for a long time. Then all of a sudden here comes this smart, gorgeous woman who's going to be working in your office. It threw you off your game, and that pissed you off. You'd rather be aggravated at her and convince yourself you didn't like her than deal with what you were actually feeling."

"That's so juvenile. It's like little kids who pull girls' hair because they like them."

"I mean. Yeah. Sort of. But that's what guys do. You might not be eight years old anymore, but you're still a guy. You don't want to face the possibility of getting hurt again, so you shoved her away before she could get close. Unfortunately, you didn't keep shoving and the attraction won out."

I still thought it sounded completely juvenile the next morning when I got to work, but I was pretty sure Cole was right. My track record with women wasn't good, and when I let myself, I could still feel the bitterness of the ones who used me before. I didn't want that to happen again, and as soon as I saw Merry, I felt a snap of need for her. The attraction was immediate and strong, going beyond just thinking she was beautiful to craving to know more about her. Just that was enough to get my guard up and make me want to push back against that feeling as hard as I could. I didn't want anything to do with her. If I just convinced her of that, eventually the feeling would wear off.

At least, that's what I told myself. And yet, here I was. Sitting in the office, wondering what the hell I was supposed to do next. I had to talk to her. That was obvious. This wasn't a television show or bad movie where we could just pretend nothing happened and go on about our lives to a soundtrack of sappy, watered-down music. We had to be upfront and honest about the situation and talk our way through it. It wasn't going to be a pleasant conversation. Definitely not one I was excited to have, but one that had to happen. If it didn't, we'd be stuck in a never-ending cycle of awkwardness.

The reality was, I had no idea what was going on in Merry's mind or what she might think was going to happen moving forward. I needed to cut off any thoughts at the pass and make sure she knew I wasn't going to fire her. Even more, I needed her to know I wasn't going to pursue her, either. Neither one was an option. Mom would strangle me bare-handed if she thought I had it in me to toss Merry aside after something happened between us. But she was possibly also capable of the same reaction if she knew I was as reckless and unprofessional as I had been at the bar.

As much as I didn't want to think about it, I knew there was a chance Merry could react badly to the whole situation. It was entirely possible she could have woken up, realized what happened, and felt like I took advantage of her. That was the last thing I wanted to happen. Not just because I would never want her to feel that way about me, but also because I didn't want her to be angry and press sexual assault charges. That was a looming thought that made my stomach turn.

I hung around in the breakroom at the beginning of the day, answering emails on my phone and listening. It was somewhat creepy in that I was all but stalking her, but I wanted to be able to start the conversation as soon as she got into work. The earlier we could get it over with, the sooner the questions would stop rolling through my mind and the tense feeling would leave my stomach.

I heard the telltale sounds of Merry coming in for the day and settling into her office. I gave her a few moments so she didn't feel like I was just springing it on her when she wasn't prepared. Not that this was the type of conversation you could really prepare for. When it sounded like she was ready for the day, I got a cup of coffee for her and walked into her office.

"Good morning," I said.

Merry looked up at me, gasping and jumping slightly. There was a startled look in her eyes, and I realized it was part from me just popping in on her, and part from something else. I hated that. Hated that she felt that and hated even more that it was my fault.

"Hi," she managed to get out.

"Can we talk?" I asked.

She nodded and gestured toward the chair across from her. I stepped further into the office and closed the door behind me. Nobody else needed to hear this conversation. Brandon was the only other person from the office who knew what had happened between Merry and me, and I doubted her brother was going to spend his first day of work spreading gossip about his little sister and the boss around the complex. I offered her the cup of coffee, and she took it from my hand, being careful not to let her fingers touch my skin.

"Thank you," she said.

"I'm just going to go ahead and jump right in. We both know what happened at the bar," I started. She drew in a breath, straightening and sitting up higher in her chair. It looked like she was about to say something, but I launched further before she could get a chance, wanting to make sure she heard what I was planning on saying before she said anything. "I just wanted to say, no harm, no foul."

That wasn't exactly the way I planned on saying it, but the words tumbled out before I could figure out a better way.

"What?" Merry asked.

"I mean, nothing is going to happen to you. Your job is

safe, your place on the team is safe. No one is going to think about you any differently, mostly because no one has to know about it. We're just going to chalk it up to too much beer and not handling our alcohol as well as we thought we could," I explained.

Merry huffed out a soft laugh, and I figured that was good. I had done my job.

20

MERRY

That was it. After all the worry and building myself up for what I had assumed was going to end up being some sort of showdown between the two of us, or at the very least, me apologizing profusely, it was all over. The conversation took only a matter of moments, and Quentin had been almost dismissive about the situation. Somehow it had all worked out, and I didn't even have to throw myself at his feet and beg for mercy. I never even got to the point of attempting to sound logical and in control of the situation. He had swept in and made everything okay. I was speechless and didn't know how to react. He offered me a smile and headed toward the door.

I watched him go to leave and knew I couldn't just let the conversation drop. As much as it was a good idea for us to just put it behind us and chalk it up to a one-night lapse in judgment like he suggested, it felt like there were still things unspoken. I needed him to understand how thankful I was that he was reacting that way and also just for what he and the rest of the company meant to my life.

I moved around the desk and took a step toward him.

"Quentin," I said to stop him.

He turned back around and looked at me.

"Yes?"

I took another step toward him and reached out to touch his arm.

"Thank you," I said. "I just wanted to thank you again for... everything. Especially for this. I've been so worried."

He nodded, but his expression hadn't changed. His eyes were locked on my lips, and I watched his shoulders square as he drew in a deep breath. I didn't have time to think about anything else.

"Fuck it," he murmured.

There was no chance to respond before he wrapped the arm I touched around my waist and pulled me in close against him. His mouth dropped down onto mine, and he kissed me deeply. The pressure of his arm around my waist guided me backward toward the door, and I heard the click of the lock.

I moved to step back, to gain some space and break the kiss that I knew if I stayed in, I would lose all control because of. But he stepped with me, and our lips never parted. I melted into the moment, aware of only the passion that was rising through my body and the butterflies in my belly. His pulled me up and into him, and I stood on my toes as he lifted me easily and carried me backward. Our movement stopped when we reached my desk, and I reached behind me to push the assortment of pens and papers away.

All rational thought tumbled out of my mind as his lips left mine and trailed down my neck. My legs spread open, and he pushed himself between them and I could feel his stiff erection through his slacks. It pushed against my hot core, and I was suddenly desperate to have him inside of me. I reached up and yanked on his tie, loosening it enough for me to get to the button at his neck. Our lips met again, and I worked my fingers down his chest, opening his shirt with a frenzied need to feel his skin. His hands had reached around me, unbuttoning the button at the top of the dress behind my neck and then pulling at the zipper down my back. The merest touch of his fingers on my spine made me break out in goosebumps. He ground his hips into mine as he pulled on the shoulders of my dress, and I leaned back to let him pull it down. As it fell to my waist, he spared no time unclipping the bra in the front clasp and pushing the cups aside to let my heavy breasts tumble out into the cool air of the office.

My nipples were hard and erect, and he took one into his mouth immediately. I moaned at the warmth and strength of his tongue on my body and arched backward, letting one hand drop to his crotch. I massaged his cock through his slacks and reached for his zipper, pulling it down in one motion and biting my lower lip. Eagerly I slid my fingers inside and found my prize. Grabbing his shaft, I pulled his long, thick cock out of his pants and wrapped my fingers around it, stroking him.

He had moved his mouth to my other breast, massaging the first with his hands, but now he moved a trail of kisses down my stomach. Kneeling on the floor, he reached up and grasped the lacy white panties I wore underneath the sundress and pulled them off before flinging them aside. I opened myself to him, prepared for him to take me there, but he stayed on his knees. Pulling my hips toward him, he dove down into my core, his tongue sweeping over me and eliciting a gasp. I lay back and rested my thighs on his shoulders as he explored me with his mouth and then a finger. At first it gently pushed into my wet pussy, but when he felt how ready for him that I was, he plunged it in, and his tongue found my clit. I writhed on the desk, and my legs clasped over his head as he lavished me with attention, and I felt the wave of an incredible orgasm crashing down over me.

With my legs shaking and my body twisted and clutched in the throes of a climax, he stood, keeping a thumb pressed into my pearl. I closed my eyes and focused on the sensation of the head of his cock brushing against my opening. He pressed the tip into me, covering it with my slick juices, and moved forward. I clutched the side of the desk with one hand and the back with the other as he slowly slid the rest of his thick, throbbing cock into me. I tried to cry out, but the sound wouldn't come, and I stayed with my mouth open as he entered me fully, stretching me and bringing me to the line between pleasure and pain. He held himself there for a moment, letting me adjust to him, to mold myself around him, and then he slid back and then even deeper inside of me.

His thumb continued to press into my clit, but now it swirled ever so gently, and the other hand cupped my breast, mimicking the motion on my nipple. He began a rhythm, first just easily sliding deep into me, but then increasing his speed so he was slamming into me, pushing against my walls and making me cry out with every thrust. My legs wrapped around him, and my ankles crossed as he fucked me, and I lost myself in my senses. His dark, sultry musk filled my nose as he hovered over me, hungrily taking my breast into his mouth, and I let one hand fill with his hair.

Suddenly, his hands reached around me, one cupping my ass and the other in the center of my back as he lifted me into the air. Guiding me with his hand, he kept me bouncing on him as he stood, and I felt weightless in his strong arms. I let one leg drop to the ground to take some of my weight off him, but let the other curl around him as he started plunging into me again, his cock filling me in ways I had never imagined. But he broke our embrace, stepping back, and I felt the emptiness of my body when he was no longer inside me. I was about to protest when he took me by my shoulders and turned me. Pushing me down into my desk, he bent me over it, and I eagerly positioned myself for him again.

His cock slid along the crack of my ass and settled at my opening before thrusting back into me. I let out a yelp of pleasure at the new sensation, and my eyes rolled back as the impending climax began to build. His thrusts were faster now, more needful, more animalistic as he took me, dominated me, and pressed me down into the desk. One hand slid up my neck and grabbed a handful of hair while the other wrapped around one of my breasts and massaged as he slammed into me. He was curled over me, and I was lost in my orgasm, incapable of thought other than pleasure, of sound other than moans, and his voice broke through. A deep growl as he got faster, harder, more intense. The sexiness of that sound drove me deeper into the unfathomable orgasm, and I cried out again. His voice matched mine, and his body locked up, thrusting one last time deep into me as he came hard. A few more pumps of his hips let him spill into me, and my body milked him empty.

21

QUENTIN

What the fuck did we just do?

The second it was over, reality sank in. That wasn't a fantasy or a dream, it actually happened, and I needed to get out of that office as fast as I could. Fortunately, Merry seemed to have the same thought. Without even a word, we disentangled ourselves from each other and got dressed. Just past the door, I heard footsteps of people showing up to work, going down the hallway, getting coffee. They had no idea what just happened. At least, I hoped with everything in me they had no idea. The last thing I needed right now was for anybody at the complex to know that I had just fucked Merry in her office.

I couldn't call attention to it. I couldn't make a scene and make anyone notice me burst out of Merry's office and rush to mine. Not that it would be out of the ordinary for me to be in her office. Everybody knew we had regular meetings to talk about the social media campaigns and the plans for upcoming posts. They wouldn't see anything strange about us meeting up on a Monday morning to lay out the week ahead. Especially considering it was a race week and we wanted to drum up as big an audience as possible and let people know about the tailgating event we were hosting before the race itself.

And that's exactly what I wanted everybody to think. When I walked out of her office, I wanted to look as usual and normal as possible so if anybody happened to be in the hallway or caught sight of me on my way to my office, it wouldn't strike them as strange in any way. Smoothing my hair and straightening my clothes to ensure they looked in place and not like I had just thrown them on, I turned to Merry. This was one of those moments where I should say something. That would just be the right thing to do. But there were literally no words that came to mind.

What would be the right thing to say at that particular moment?

"I have a lot of work to do," Merry finally said.

Thankful that I didn't have to come up with something clever, I nodded and walked out, smiling at Darren when he came out of the breakroom with a cup of coffee.

"Hey," he said. "Didn't expect to see you here."

"What do you mean?" I asked, hoping not to sound defensive.

"You're usually already in your office nursing your third cup by now. Unless Mom is freaking out, then you're in the breakroom stealing a cinnamon bun or muffin," he said.

I forced myself to relax and laugh.

"It's a race week, so I'm sure she'll be channeling her very best Betty Crocker by the middle of the day. I'm saving myself," I told him. "Maybe she'll make that chocolate cherry cake thing she does sometimes."

"Text me the second you find out," he said seriously.

I nodded. "You have my word."

"All right. I'm going to head down to the track. Do a few practice runs."

"I'll be down later to watch," I said.

My little brother held up his cup of coffee.

"You should grab a cup. You look a little out of it."

He walked toward the door to the outside, and I continued toward my office, keeping it together, not speeding up or letting my expression reveal anything. I managed to make it all the way to my office before freaking out. I considered that a massive accomplishment. By the time I walked through the door, I felt like I was going to crack. When it closed behind me, I did.

I dug my fingers back through my hair and let out a sound somewhere between a growl and a gasp. I couldn't believe I'd just done that. That morning when I got up, I was on the brink of completely freaking out because I didn't know what was going through her mind or what I was supposed to say to her. I'd stood there in the breakroom waiting for her to come to work so I could talk to her about kissing her in the bar. I was so worked up about kissing her, just kissing her, I'd thought about it every second until I got into her office to talk to her about it.

Then I stood there and promised her that her job was safe. I reassured her I wasn't going to do anything to let anybody know what happened and that we could just forget it. That was supposed to be where it ended. She'd looked so happy, and I knew I'd done the right thing. Then she had to come around that desk and touch my arm the way she did. Anybody else would have been able to just deal with it, but not me. I freaking pounced on her. Not thirty seconds after pushing the reset button and clearing the air so we could have just gone on like everything was fine, I grabbed her and kissed her. Five more steps. If I had just taken five more steps, I would have gotten out of the office and could have gone about my day like normal.

Instead, I kissed her. And then I fucked her. In her office. Right there on her desk with the rest of the complex going on like business as usual. In all the years I'd worked at the complex, that wasn't even something that crossed my mind.

Shit. If Mom found out, she was going to castrate me.

Mom knew this was my company, and she respected me as the head of it. She'd watched me build it and was extremely proud of me for what I'd accomplished. But in her heart, this was still in so many ways my father's company. He never wanted it to be big like I did. It was just something small he carried on after sharing a love of racing his own father. But I knew how much she respected the business and how sacred she thought every inch of the complex was. If she knew not only that I'd had sex in one of the offices, but that it was with an employee and during business hours, she would never get over it. That would push her right over the edge.

I had to fix this. Somehow, I had to deal with what happened and get us back to that reset button so we could move forward. But it was obvious I couldn't do it in person. I had developed a very strong taste for Merry that I apparently had no capacity to resist. Just being in the same space with her made me completely lose control of myself. My mind stopped working clearly, and my body took over. That meant going to her office again to try to talk this out was just a really bad idea. The last thing I needed right then was to stroll back in there with all the intention in the world of apologizing and clearing the air again, only to go for round two.

An email was seriously my only option at that point. I

pulled one up and stared at the blank white box for a long time trying to figure out the exact words. I typed out several messages only to erase them and go back to staring. For someone who sent dozens of emails on a normal day, this was really freaking difficult. Of course, this was the first time I'd ever had to send this particular style of email. Some of the messages seemed way too long and complex, turning the situation into something bigger and more dramatic than I needed to make it. Others were too curt and short, sounding dismissive and possibly even cruel. There had to be some sort of happy medium.

Finally, I settled on a message that was basic and straightforward, but hopefully not too cold. In it, I apologized for letting myself get carried away and not stopping myself. Then I promised I would stay out of her way at all times unless it was strictly necessary for work, and reiterated she was definitely not going to lose her job. It still felt strange and not exactly right, but I couldn't keep letting myself go over it and over it. If I did, I would spend the entire day trying to make it perfect. That just wasn't an option. I needed to send it and be done with it. Before I could second-guess myself again, I pressed Send, then settled into the uncomfortable period of waiting for a response.

If one came. It was entirely possible she would just read the email, delete it, and go about her life pretending like nothing happened and never acknowledge it. I didn't know if that would be better or worse than getting something back from her. When a response popped into my inbox, I felt my chest tighten. But it was only one line.

"I won't tell if you don't."

That was enough. It wasn't emotional or personal, but it also didn't feel like blackmail, so I was okay with that.

For the rest of the day, I did exactly what I'd promised in the email and steered absolutely clear of Merry. We didn't have one of our meetings scheduled until the end of the week. That seemed like an oversight at the beginning of that day, but now it was a blessing. We would have a couple of days to let everything settle down, and then we could attempt the whole "normal" thing. In the afternoon, I headed down to the practice track and watched Darren do laps for a while. He pushed his bike to its new limits, testing out the modifications made since the last race.

After a while, Greg joined him and they went around in circles, chasing each other, battling for position. It was exciting to watch, but also a little nerve-racking. The reality of having two riders in the race was stronger now that we were approaching the second race. It was a novelty for the first one of the season. We'd never had two riders in a race, and it was a thrill thinking about going after two positions. Then it felt like it was the two of them against the rest of the teams. That had changed this week. Now it felt like the two of them were against each other, and that put new pressure on both, and on the whole team. But I welcomed it. At least it was something to think about other than how much I wanted to have Merry over and over again.

22

MERRY

I sat at my desk Tuesday, staring blankly at my computer. I could barely think straight. The whole mess with Quentin was hanging over me, and I felt like the world was pressing in on me from all sides.

I still couldn't believe I'd had sex with my boss in my office. I wasn't raised like that, and it was so completely out of character, I couldn't even wrap my head around it. Up until that morning, I didn't think I'd ever even considered that people actually did that in real life. Movies and TV shows, absolutely. But not in the real world. And definitely not in *my* life.

Unable to concentrate, I ended up spinning around in the chair, staring up at the ceiling. The longer I sat in the office, the more the memories of what happened there the day before caused heat to burn across my cheeks and my heart to flutter in my chest. I felt like a crazy person. I wanted to put the entire thing behind me, but I couldn't keep the memories from rushing through my brain.

I needed to get over it. This was not the time for me to get distracted and be unable to focus on what was in front of me. There was way too much for me to be doing to spend my day spinning around in a desk chair contemplating my boss's body and how it felt on mine. I really needed to get to work if I was going to even get close to accomplishing the goals I had for drumming up interest in the race the next night.

But it wasn't just the race itself I was promoting. The tailgating event being hosted in the parking lot before the race itself was my idea. During one of my meetings with Quentin, I'd suggested putting together an event outside of the traditional race experience to let fans get more up close and personal with the team and also socialize with each other. The more energy and excitement we could build up, and the more of a bonded atmosphere we could create among the fans, the fiercer the loyalty and devotion there would be. And that meant more ticket sales, more merchandise sales, more successful appearances, and a bigger presence online. In order for that to work, I needed to spread the word and get as many people interested in coming as possible.

The company was already popular, and the fan base was there. Now it was a matter of taking what was already successful and crank up the visibility, power, and reach. Quentin's millions were evidence the potential was there. If it was tapped, the effect could be astounding.

I was able to push the memories into the back of my mind by midmorning and bury myself in work. I didn't come up for air until I heard a knock on my door, and my heart jumped into my throat. Fortunately, when I croaked out for the person to come in, it was Brandon's face that popped into my office.

"Ready for lunch?" he asked.

"Absolutely," I told him. "I didn't even realize it was getting so late. I'm starving."

"Great. What are you thinking?" he asked.

"Actually, I want to introduce you to the place we get food from usually a couple of times a week," I said. "It's a little box lunch place not too far from here. We can call and have it delivered, then go outside and eat."

"That sounds perfect," Brandon said.

It didn't take long for the food to be delivered, and we brought it outside to sit under the tree I'd become so fond of during the time I worked there. Before the food got there, I had sent Brandon out to the car to grab the blanket I kept in the trunk for occasions just like this.

We spread the blanket out across the grass and unpacked our lunches. The first few moments were spent in the time-honored sibling tradition of dividing up food and trading items so we could each build our own ideal lunch.

"So, how has your first day been?" I asked, plucking the pickle slice from my little white paper cup of the best potato salad I'd ever tasted and popping it in my mouth.

"Really great. Everybody is so nice here. I already feel really welcome, and since I spent all that time with Artie, everything is smooth and pretty easy so far," he told me.

"That's good to hear. I told you the people here were awesome. That's why I was so glad you got the job. It's a great place to work."

"You sound like a promotional brochure," he said with a laugh as he picked up his cold roast beef sandwich for a bite.

I nodded. "I feel kind of like one. It's the marketing side of doing social media. The company doesn't have a real marketing department, so it's just me."

"How is that possible?" Brandon asked. "It's not like it's a tiny, unknown company. How did it get this far?"

"Quentin," I answered simply. "Up until now he's handled things like getting local sponsors and spreading the news about races and things by word of mouth. I think that's a big reason why he was so resistant to the idea of adding a big social media push to the company. He likes feeling like his fandom was built organically and that he's still a hometown boy. So, that's what I'm trying to do with the campaign. Be impressive and humble at the same time."

"Good luck with that one," Brandon said. "Sounds like you're taking on more for this company than you ever have."

"Most definitely. But I knew that going in. That's part of why I was so excited to get a consistent, secure position rather than all that gig work. Working here really lets me get into the meat of it and do more. It's exciting. I just hope I'm doing well and don't end up completely flopping," I admitted.

"You're not going to flop. You don't have it in you to flop," he said.

"You're supposed to say that. You're my big brother," I smiled. "We'll see tomorrow at this tailgating thing. There's been good interest, and I'm looking forward to seeing how it plays out. If it does well and we can get more attention, we might be able to land bigger sponsors."

"I'm sure people will love it. And Quentin is going to be even happier with you than he already is," he said.

"What do you mean by that?" I asked, realizing only after the words came out of my mouth how snappy and defensive they sounded.

My brother stared at me as if I had three heads.

"Um. That he's happy with your performance at your

job?" he asked. His eyes searched my face. "Is there something else I could have meant by that?"

The images I'd been trying to chase out of my mind came rushing back, and I did my best not to think about them.

"Nope," I said. "Of course not. You're planning on coming to the race, aren't you?"

He ate his sandwich, his expression showing how thrown off he was by the breakneck change in direction I took the conversation.

"I am," he said.

"Great. We'll drive in together and you can go to the tailgating event with me. Then we'll sit in the company box with Minnie," I said.

We finished up our lunch talking about the upcoming race, then went back to our offices where I slumped against the desk, embarrassed by my close call of almost revealing everything to my brother.

23

QUENTIN

Race days were simultaneously my favorite and least favorite days of the season. They were always, in a word, a mess. Everywhere all over the complex, people were running around like crazy, tempers flaring as they scrambled to get things done. No matter how much we prepared and how much time we put into getting everything ready, the morning of a race day always came with what seemed like an insurmountable list of tasks to complete and preparations to make in time for the event. And now with the added pressures of our first tailgating party, it seemed like there simply weren't enough hours in the day for us to be completely ready.

When Merry had made the suggestion about the tailgating event, it sounded like a fantastic idea. Fans already liked to gather in the parking lots before the race, playing music, cooking food, and getting a few drinks in before loading into the stands. For some, the party just kept rolling. They didn't even bother to go into the stands and instead parked on the hills that surrounded the track so they could look down over the action and keep their raucous entertainment going throughout. Hosting our own event would bring attention to our team, make the fans feel special, and get the energy going so they would be even more excited to be there.

Merry and Mom had been working together designing special merchandise for the party. They hadn't shown me any of the finalized designs yet, but I knew Mom was waiting anxiously for four boxes to be delivered. There was supposed to be here yesterday, but they never made it. They needed to get here quickly if the team was going to have enough time to bring them down to the track and get them set up with the rest of the party. That in and of itself was creating more anxiety and frantic energy throughout the complex. We were all excited about the party, but at the same time it was new, and we didn't really know what to expect. The reality of taking time away from being down at the track gearing up for the race was starting to creep in for me. I was used to being there well ahead of time, tweaking the bikes and getting an overview of the track conditions. I'd still have time to do that but making an appearance at the party would cut into it. I had to see how I was able to balance the two to determine if this was something we could do again.

But it wasn't just normal pre-race jitters and stress that was getting to me. I was dealing with a secret—a big secret, and I hated it. Honesty was always a big thing for my family. From the time I was a small child, my parents instilled in me that honesty was one of the most important personal characteristics anyone could have. Even if you were wrong about something or made a mistake, being honest about it prevented the situation from being worse. That was dragging me down as I carried around the biggest secret I ever had. Knowing how disappointed they would be in me not just for what I did, but for being dishonest about it, was getting to me. Keeping something from them at all was hard, but keeping something like this, something potentially harmful to the company, a secret, was taking its toll on me.

I felt like I couldn't get my brain wrapped around what I was supposed to be doing. Even though I'd done this dozens of times before, I couldn't think straight. I couldn't make myself finish any task or get anything done. All of it had me walking along the complex feeling lost, unsure of what I was supposed to do next. I was so out of it I didn't even notice my father come around the corner directly at me. He tried to move out of my way, but we ended up running into each other, and all the papers and my tablet I was carrying in my arms toppled to the floor and spilled out around me. The sound shocked me back into reality, and I shook my head to get the fog away.

Dad wrapped his arm around my shoulders and patted my back.

"Everything okay, my boy?" he asked.

Just the fact that he asked that told me he already knew there was something going on. That was my father's way. He could tell when there was something wrong with one of his sons, but he was never the kind to push or pry. He would give each of us our own time and space to tell him what was on our minds, then help us in any way he could. I wanted to pour out everything to him and let him make me feel better, but at the same time I knew I couldn't. I needed to get away from him as quickly as I could. I didn't have it in me not to open up to him if he kept asking.

I bent down and scooped up everything from the floor, nodding but not saying anything until I was sure I had myself together.

"Just trying to get ready for the race," I told him. "There's a lot going on today."

He chuckled. "You're telling me. Your mother has asked me about a thousand times if that delivery has gotten here yet. If it doesn't get here pretty soon, I think she's going to end up trying to walk her way around the truck's route to find them."

I forced a laugh.

"Sounds like Mom," I said.

Just as I said it, his phone alerted him to a new message, and he looked down at it.

"Speak of the devil," he said. "I better get up there and help her unload. Have you eaten today? You're looking kind of pale. Make sure you're not so focused on everything you forget to take care of yourself. Go by the kitchen and grab something your mother made. She was on a savory kick this morning. The rosemary and cheese bread is really good."

"I will," I reassured him.

I was relieved when he finally walked away and I could duck into an empty office, taking a few deep breaths to ease my shaking. I couldn't keep going like this. There was no way I was going to be able to keep this locked up inside me and just expect it to dissolve away eventually so I could pretend it didn't happen. As much as that's what I wanted, or at least what I told myself I wanted, it wasn't realistic. Not for me. I couldn't keep pretending. It felt like a lie, and that wasn't something I could handle.

I needed to talk to Merry. I knew what I'd said to her and what she was probably thinking. It wouldn't be easy to have the conversation we needed to have, but it had to be done. I had never been good at secrets, and I wasn't about to let this one ruin my life. We needed to talk it out and figure out how we were really going to handle it.

Resolute in what we needed to do, I headed to Merry's office. She was inside packing up her go-to bag of electronics.

"Hey," I said as I walked through the open door.

She looked up at me with a guarded expression.

"Hi," she said.

"We need to talk," I told her.

She nodded but didn't stop loading her bag.

"Okay, but I really can't right now," she said.

"You can't right now?" I asked, a little surprised.

She nodded again as she added a file folder and notebook into her bag and slipped it over her shoulder.

"Brandon is waiting for me. We have to get down to the track and start setting up for the tailgate event. There's a lot to do and not a lot of time to do it. Since we weren't able to go there over the weekend or earlier this week and look over everything to try to figure out the logistics of setting up, it's going to be more of a crunch to get ready before the fans get there," she said.

She headed out of her office, and I fell into step beside her.

"Merry, this is really serious. We have to talk about what happened," I said.

"I thought we agreed that was over and done with, and behind us," she said.

"We did, but I've been thinking about it, and that's just not going to be possible," I told her.

"I'm sorry, Quentin, but I really can't talk about this right now. I need to get to the track, get everything set up, and make sure the party goes well. You should be thinking about that, too. You know the fans are coming out to see the team," she said.

Before I could say any more, we walked outside, and

Brandon was standing there waiting for her. He smiled broadly and came toward us.

"Hey, sis. Hey, Quentin," he said.

"Hi, Brandon," I said. "Settling in all right?"

"Yes. It's been great so far. Thanks. Are you excited about the race tonight?" he asked.

"Absolutely," I told him. "In fact, your sister and I were just talking about the tailgate party."

"It should be fun. I'm really looking forward to the whole thing," he said.

"We should actually get going," Merry said. "We don't have any time to waste. See you there, Quentin."

She hurried away with her brother scurrying to catch up with her. He leaned in close to mutter something to her that I couldn't hear, but all she did was shake her head and keep rushing toward the parking lot. I watched her go, knowing I couldn't just let this drop. It was going to push me over the edge if I kept trying to just go on like nothing happened.

It was almost three hours later when I managed to get near Merry again. I stayed behind at the complex for a while after she left to finish up what needed to be done and help load everything on the trucks. By the time we got to the track, we had little time to unload and get to the tailgate. As soon as we arrived, we were swept up into the fun, which was just what we all wanted. She had really done an exceptional job putting everything together, and I was impressed from the local food truck cooking to one side with the DJ playing music, to the merchandise stand and the areas set up for the team to take pictures and sign autographs. I made my appearance and did what I needed to do, then caught sight of her lingering by herself near the merchandise table.

Moving quickly, I got to the table and reached out to touch her arm.

"Merry, we need to talk," I said. "The party is in full swing, and everyone is doing great. We can talk for a few minutes before we need to get down to the track."

She looked like she was trying to come up with an excuse to get away from me again, but when nothing came to mind, she gave a reluctant nod.

"All right," she said.

"Let's go to the company box. There won't be anybody there yet," I said.

I walked away from the crowd with Merry by my side and knowing I had only a few minutes to figure out exactly what I was going to say to her when we got to the box.

24

MERRY

"I don't think I can keep doing this," Quentin said.

"What do you mean?" I asked. "Do what?"

"I can't keep pretending nothing happened between us," he started.

"But that's what we said we were going to do," I cut him off. "As soon as it happened, we both knew it was a mistake and we needed to move past it. We agreed to just pretend it didn't happen so we could keep going without there being any awkwardness."

I felt like I was getting shrill and knew I was repeating myself. He wasn't looking convinced, and maybe if I just reiterated the same things over and over, they'd sink in and we could just head back to the event for a convivial hamburger and soda before the race. As soon as I stopped talking, though, I knew that wasn't going to happen. There were still words on his lips, and I wasn't going to get out of hearing them.

"I thought I was going to be able to do that, but I can't. My family is extremely close, and I don't keep things from them. It's especially hard to do that in this particular situation considering we work together and most of my family is there with us," he said.

"So, what do you want to do?" I asked. "Put out a bulletin in the company newsletter that we had sex in my office?"

"I don't think it needs to go that far," he said. "I know this isn't the easiest situation for you, either. But just hear me out. We don't need to present it as we just got swept up and made an impulsive decision. Instead, we put a spin on it."

"A spin?" I asked.

"Yes. We say we had a fling. Present it as there was something there and we made an intentional decision to spend time together, but then we both realized it wasn't going to go anywhere, so we let it drop. It's not a big deal, and we're perfectly fine with each other. There aren't any hard feelings or issues between us," he said. "We just get it all out in the open, and that way we're not trying to hide anything or going behind anybody's back."

I thought about that for a few seconds. That actually didn't sound so bad. But there were still some sticky questions that needed to be managed.

"Isn't that going to cause problems, though? The boss sleeping with his employee? Even if it was a fling?" I asked.

Quentin shook his head.

"No. The company doesn't have any rules about fraternization. That's actually a throwback to when my father owned it. He always had the joke that because he owned the company and was married to the woman who did the hiring, he couldn't have rules against intra-office relationships because then he'd have to fire himself since he certainly wasn't going to stop fraternizing with his wife."

Finally, I nodded.

"That could definitely work," I agreed. "I've actually been wanting to tell my best friend about it, just because like you said, I didn't want to just have it all locked up inside. But I decided against it because I didn't really know how it would come across. But if we're going to put that spin on it, then it's fine."

We talked for another few seconds, then headed back. I felt better as we walked together toward the party, ready to send the team off to prepare for the race to begin. There was a strange sense of weight being lifted off of me. Up until that moment, I didn't realize the situation was bothering me any more than just being shocked and a little dismayed by my own decision making. It didn't occur to me that not being able to talk to anyone about it was a problem. Not talking to Olivia was unusual, but only because I talked to her about everything.

Now that Quentin and I had talked, though, I realized it was getting to me more than I would have expected. Having a way to talk about it openly, and just knowing what to say about it if anyone was to confront me about it, seemed like it would help. At least now I was prepared and not in some strange middle ground where my official stance was that it just didn't happen at all. Really thinking about it, that all felt a bit too UFO-classified-files to me, and it was much more natural to be able to tell people without the weirdness.

It was also a relief just to hear him say we weren't breaking any rules. I'd never worked for a company that didn't clearly and intensely lay out restrictions for employees dating, especially if it involved people at different levels of the hierarchy. That's what scared me the most and hearing they didn't have those regulations put my mind at ease. We didn't do anything against policy, which meant he didn't have to choose between firing me or giving me preferential treatment, either of which would be awkward.

After the emotion, tension, and eventual tremendous relief of the talk with Quentin, I didn't have nearly as much anticipation for the race. Watching dozens of motorcycles fly around the track didn't have the same excitement and adrenaline as getting things out in the open and finalizing that things were really going to work out. That almost felt like an afterthought. Especially when it got right down to the performance of the team.

The first race of the season was almost overwhelming. I'd never watched anything like that and felt right on the edge from the second the engines roared, and the bikes took off from the starting line. Darren and Greg were almost flawless in their runs and battled to the very end, creating an almost painful amount of anticipation that kept me on my feet.

It didn't feel like that this time. It was still exciting, and I cheered them on from my spot in between Minnie and Brandon, but there was definitely something off about this run. Greg performed well, his bike obviously improved and his confidence even stronger this time. He shot out to the front right from the beginning, only trailing Darren. At first it seemed there would be no competition. These two would simply glide to the finish and it would be done.

Then the other teams started gaining on them. Rather than there being a clearly defined ranking, there was a crush of bikes shifting up and down as they spiraled around the track. After several laps, Greg came out in front again. Darren slid up behind him, and another two teams gained on them. Darren and Greg both inched ahead, and for the next several laps, there was little change. It looked like they were just riding around in circles. As the final stretch of the race approached, I left the company box and headed down toward the rest of the team. Using credentials Gus gave to me earlier, I got into the secure area and went to join the others waiting for the end. It was obvious our two riders were going to come out on top, and I wanted to be as close as possible to capture the victory.

Then something suddenly changed. Greg and Darren were jockeying for first place when a bike came up behind Darren and swerved too close. He shifted to get out of the way, but the positioning was too tight, and the rider clipped his tire. He managed to stay upright but slid across the track, allowing Greg to jump forward and losing valuable seconds. I snapped picture after picture of Greg winning first position but gasped as Darren toppled, the wreck shoving him over the line in fifth place.

Quentin and the rest of the team ran toward him, but when I saw him get up and let out an angry yell, I knew he was all right. I needed to turn my attention to the celebration at the finish line. I live-tweeted the excitement, capturing as much of Greg's thrill at his first win as I could while people rushed in around him to congratulate him. After a few seconds, Darren, Quentin, and the rest of the team joined us. Darren graciously congratulated Greg, but I could tell he was furious.

When some of the chaos died down, I went over to Darren. Patting my friend on the back, I leaned in so he would be able to hear me.

"You doing okay?" I asked. "That looked like a nasty skid."

"I'm all right," he said. "I'll probably be sore as hell for the next few days, but it looked worse than it was. I'm just pissed I lost my position because of that asshole. That wreck was totally Austin's fault. It wasn't even a mistake. It was just really bad riding. He could have killed someone out there just because he doesn't know how to control himself."

"I'm sorry. Hopefully he learns his lesson."

When the post-race celebration died down, Brandon and I headed home, dissecting the race and everything that happened. I didn't let him know how I was feeling. He'd enjoyed the experience, so I didn't want to dampen his spirits by letting him know how anticlimactic the race seemed.

25

QUENTIN

The team went to the bar to celebrate Greg's win, but didn't have the same energy as the first race. Even Greg didn't seem as interested in being there as before. He was much more interested in going home and getting some rest. He'd put himself through the wringer trying to get ready for this race, now that it was over and he accomplished his goal, he wanted some downtime. Instead of us staying out late and not starting work until after lunch the next day, I decided to trim down the rest of the week. As soon as I got home after the brief celebration at the bar, I sent out a group text to everyone on the crew letting them know we were going to take half days on both Thursday and Friday. That would give us time to do the usual post-race evaluations but let us get in some relaxation as well.

Thursday was almost methodical. I hadn't bothered to unload the trucks after the race, so we spent the first couple of hours after getting into the complex breaking down and getting everything put away. I then met with Greg to personally congratulate him and talk about what was next. He was already looking ahead to the next race but was happy to have a couple of days where there wasn't as much pressure. He looked forward to spending Thursday morning cleaning his bike and going over maintenance and repair needs with the team of mechanics, then planned to spend Friday meeting with a physical trainer at the complex gym. Now that he felt his bike was in peak condition, he wanted to focus on his body. Doing CrossFit like Darren didn't appeal to Greg. He was much more the traditional cardio and weight training type. But that's why I kept several different physical trainers on retainer. It meant anyone on the team, but especially the riders, could make sure they were taking care of their health.

Next, I checked in on Darren. I found him just like I had after the first race, standing in the middle of the garage surrounded by the parts of his dismantled bike.

"Wow," I said. "Twice in a row. Getting serious this time."

"The wreck did a little bit of damage," he said. "And I want to see if there's anything that can be done to stabilize it more. I thought the modifications we made after last race would make it safer and more responsive, but apparently not so much."

"You know that wreck wasn't your fault. And the fact that you stayed up for as long as you did and didn't completely get smashed tells me the bike was performing well," I told him.

He nodded. I knew he was upset about his performance, and it would take him some time for the physical and emotional effects of it to go away. All I could do was support him.

The next day I finished up some administrative work and then headed to Cole's place. When I pulled into the driveway with lunch, I got a text telling me to come around to the back. This was the first time I'd seen the new place he got when he came back from Tibet, and I instantly saw what he liked about it. The house and the land around it was exactly what I would have pinpointed for him. It wasn't lost on me, though, that instead of choosing an apartment or something small just for him, he'd immediately chosen a house with plenty of space for a family. That was Cole. Even with the bad experience with his wife, he hadn't lost sight of the future and the possibility of someone sharing it.

When I walked through the big wooden gate leading into the backyard, I immediately saw the house wasn't the only new thing in Cole's life. He was running around with a tiny yellow puppy, laughing as he threw a ball and the puppy went after it with all his legs seeming to go in different directions.

"Hey," he called when he saw me.

We went up to the porch and spread out the food on a table with a blue-and-white striped umbrella to block the sun.

"I see you have a new friend," I said when he dropped into the seat across from me.

"Yeah. I just adopted him. I didn't even mean to. That pet supply store by the supermarket was having an adoption day and he was sitting out front when I went to grab a few things. I couldn't resist him."

Trying not to be too obvious about it, I evaluated my best friend. He looked calm and happy. It was a major improvement from the time right after the divorce when it seemed like he was going to fall apart at any moment. It was really good to have him home. There were times during those six months when I honestly thought he might not ever make it back. I hated feeling so helpless at that time, not being able to do anything to make him feel better.

It wasn't just that I didn't have the personal insight and experience. I definitely didn't. I'd never been through something even close to a divorce, so I didn't know how he felt and what might make it easier for him. But it was more than that. Just like he said, Cole needed to find himself again. He needed to figure out who he was and how he was going to move forward without his wife. That was something he had to do on his own, and there was nothing I could do to make it any better. My only option was to make sure he knew I was there for him and would be when he made it back home.

We talked about the puppy for a few more minutes, and then he asked about the race.

"It was kind of a mess, to be honest," I told him. "I mean, Greg did awesome. He came in first, and it was a really smooth race for him. But some other teams were really aggressive, and one rider caused a wreck for Darren."

"Damn. Is he doing okay?" Cole asked.

"He'll be fine," I told him.

"Sorry I missed it. Getting used to this new job is a little more complicated than I thought."

"How is it going for you?" I asked.

"Really well. I'm enjoying it. It's just getting used to how different it is than actually being in the classroom. I have to approach everything in a totally different way. I never really thought about how I'd have to change my approach to just about everything because I wasn't going to be in the classroom with the people," he told me.

"I can imagine that would take some getting used to," I said.

"How about you?" he asked. "How are you doing?"

There was something more behind that question than it

sounded. I knew he was trying to get at something but didn't want to come right out and ask.

"What do you mean?" I asked.

"You think I just forgot about what happened last weekend at the bar?" he asked. "We never talked about that."

"Do we need to? You saw it."

"Come on, Q. I know you. That wasn't just some sloppy drunken kissing. What's going on between you and that social media girl?"

"Merry," I corrected quickly, and he gave me a knowing look. I let out a sigh.

There was no real point in trying to avoid it anymore. He was going to figure out a way to get it out of me at some point anyway. If there was anyone I needed to be honest about the situation with, it was Cole. He knew me better than anybody other than my brothers, in some ways, even better because he was there at times when my brothers were away from home or I was. He would listen to me without judgment and tell me the truth.

Tossing aside the newer version of what happened between Merry and me, I laid it all out, telling him everything from start to finish. I didn't go into extreme detail, but it was enough for him to know everything he needed to. When I was finished, I leaned back in my chair, waiting for his reaction. He stared back at me without a change in emotion.

"Well," he finally said. "You had to fall at some point."

"What?" I asked.

"This was going to happen and, frankly, it's about time. Don't let my bad experience or, hell, your own bad experiences, stop you from trying for more," he said.

That hit me hard, and I let it sink in. Somehow, he knew

exactly what I was worried about, exactly how I was thinking. But it didn't matter. No matter what I was thinking or feeling, I didn't think it could go anywhere. Merry and I already agreed it was a one-and-done thing, and I had to accept that.

26

MERRY

Saturday didn't seem like it could come fast enough for me that week. Quentin told the crew they could take half days on Thursday and Friday, which meant the complex all but cleared out by noon. There really wasn't much reason for me to stay there at the office when everybody else was taking off. Mine was the kind of work essentially made for doing remotely. There was a ton for me to do following the race. I needed to post the pictures, follow up on the live stream of the celebration, and gather feedback for the tailgate event. From there I could determine which parts of my campaign had been successful so far, which could be tweaked further, and what I could add. It would also help me in planning future events. Since I was the one who suggested the party, the bulk of putting it together fell on me. Minnie was there to help, but it was an added responsibility I didn't really sign up for but enjoyed taking on.

No matter how much I needed to do, though, it didn't really require me to be in the office. With the exception of having meetings with Minnie or Quentin, I could do everything from my living room couch with my tablet in my lap and my laptop on the table in front of me if I really wanted to. Since both of them left the complex late in the morning, there were no meetings to keep me there. The only thing that had me locked in place at the office rather than heading home was knowing I probably wouldn't be able to focus at home. I was still struggling with everything that happened, and now that Brandon was sharing my apartment, it would be far more difficult to actually concentrate on what needed to be done. Honestly, it was far more likely I would end up in stretchy pants eating popcorn and getting lost in daytime TV under the guise of researching what interested our demographics than it was I'd get everything done the way I needed to.

So, I stayed at the office. All day Thursday and all day Friday, I sat behind my desk in the strangely quiet office building, straining for the sound of the mechanics or anyone else at the complex. It was a little eerie for it to be so still, but it forced me to delve into what I needed to do. And by the end of the day Friday, I was exhausted and more than ready for the weekend. Olivia and I were going to get together, and I was looking forward to that. We hadn't been able to have as much time together as we usually did, and I was missing her.

I had every intention of having her over to the house for a long day of hanging out, baking cupcakes, and girl talk. But that wasn't to be. I wasn't even out of bed Saturday morning when I heard Brandon's angry voice coming from the kitchen. It was so loud and intense I thought for a minute someone was there. I threw on my bathrobe and rushed out to check on him but found him pacing through the living room on his phone. Now that I was in the same room with him and could more clearly hear what he was saying, I knew he was talking to his ex. Unsurprisingly, it wasn't a pleasant conversation. And it didn't sound like it would be ending anytime soon.

Going back into my room, I took a shower, got dressed, and put on my makeup. I was trying to give him time and privacy, but he hadn't stopped by the time I was finished. When I got into the living room, he wrenched the phone away from his ear and stared at it in disbelief.

"What happened?" I asked.

"She hung up on me," he said angrily. "She says she's coming over here."

"What?" I asked, shocked. "Why would she do that?"

"Apparently, she's pissed about what I got from the house. She wants to come over here and talk about it, and says we need to talk about the divorce."

"What is there to talk about? You already filed papers," I said.

"There are a bunch of steps that have to be taken, and she wants to control all of them. I'm sure that doesn't come as much of a surprise," he told me.

"Do you want me here when she comes?" I asked.

As much as I wanted to see Olivia, if my brother needed me, he would have to come first. This was an extremely hard time for him, and I wanted to give them as much support as I could. But he shook his head.

"There's no need for you to get wrapped up in this. I'm sure it's not going to be a warm and fuzzy reunion and having you here would probably just make her really defensive. If it's all right with you, I'd rather just be here by myself," he told me.

"Sure. I'm going to hang out with Olivia. I'll probably be gone most of the day, but if you need me, just call. I'll get back here as fast as I can," I promised.

I headed out of the house worried about my brother and thinking about what I was going to tell Olivia. Spending time with her was about relaxing and having some fun, but it was also my chance to get the whole situation with Quentin off my chest. I needed to get it all out and let her help me work through my conflicting feelings. It seemed like she already knew something was happening in my head as soon as I walked into the small local coffee shop where we agreed to meet.

"I ordered you a latte," she said when I sat down. "What's going on?"

"You're not even going to pretend to start with small talk, are you?" I asked.

"Nope. We don't need small talk. It's you and me. We've had enough small talk to last for the rest of our lives."

"True."

"So, what's going on? Because I can see that look on your face. The gears are grinding around in your head. What's bothering you?" she asked.

"It's about my boss," I finally said.

She took a sip of her latte.

"Quentin?" she asked.

"Yes."

"What about him? Is he causing trouble because of the kissing thing?" she asked.

"Not exactly. I..." I sighed, not sure I even wanted to put a voice to the words, but knowing I needed to. "I think I might have gone ahead and caught feelings for him."

"What?" Olivia asked, sounding more confused than startled like I was expecting her to be. "You said it was just a stupid thing because you drank too much that night."

I cringed. "I know. It's all really confusing. I feel so conflicted. Ever since that night, I've been trying to just push it away and ignore it, but there are definitely feelings building. They just crept up on me, and I'm really not happy about it."

"So, that's it? You're just struggling with feelings for your boss? That's not that big of a deal," she said. "I mean, I know it probably feels really strange and might be kind of freaking you out, but I've known a lot of people who had crushes on their bosses. And Quentin is super hot. And rich. You could do a lot worse, so it makes sense you would start crushing on him, especially after he kissed you like that."

Hearing her put it out there like that both helped and made me more confused. This didn't feel like just a crush. It wasn't just a slight attraction. But she didn't know how far it had gone. I needed to think about it more before I went any further with the story.

"That makes sense," I said.

Olivia nodded. "So, how is Brandon?"

I couldn't help but smile at the question. She had always liked my brother from the time she met him but being married was obviously a deterrent to her letting him know how she felt or doing anything about it. I didn't think she was going to try to jump on the opportunity now, but it was cute to see her worrying about him and taking more interest.

"He's not great, to be honest. Just trying to get through this whole divorce thing and not fall apart. He's actually at home right now waiting for his ex to come over and talk about stuff," I told her.

"I hate that for him," Olivia said. "He's such a good guy. He really deserves somebody who will be good to him and show him how special he is..."

"I slept with Quentin."

Well, there went thinking about it some more. I didn't mean it to, but it just kind of popped out of my mouth.

"You what?" Olivia asked, now finally sounding shocked.

"I had sex with Quentin. At work. In my office," I told her.

She gasped, her hand flying up to cover her mouth.

"I think this requires some fresh air," she said after a few seconds.

We finished our drinks and headed out to walk to a nearby park where we could talk openly without anybody listening in. I didn't tell her the lie Quentin came up with. When he first said it, it made sense and I was willing to go along with it. But now that I was actually standing here with my best friend, it didn't seem right. I wanted to tell her everything. She needed to know why I was grappling with my feelings the way I was. I spilled out the whole story, and as soon as I was finished, I felt so much lighter. Even with my best friend scrambling to find the right words, it felt better to have said something.

"You don't really need to say anything right now. I'm still trying to figure it out myself. The thing is, we already agreed it wasn't going to happen again. It would only happen one time because it was a mistake, and that we have to just put it behind us. That's why the feelings are so inconvenient. Now that I've told you about it, though, I think it's going to be easier to deal with."

"Good. And you know I'm sworn to secrecy. Whatever you're going to do, you need to do it without anyone interfering. So I'm going to keep my opinions to myself for now. How about we go find some fun?"

I laughed. "That sounds like a really good idea."

She grinned and linked arms with me. We made our

way through the rest of the park, then headed for our favorite outdoor mall. We spent the rest of the day shopping and chatting about breezy, inconsequential things that let me keep my mind off everything. Dinner at a seafood restaurant was the perfect end to the day, and I went home feeling much better.

27

QUENTIN

My first meeting of the day Monday morning was with Brandon. I scheduled it right after he was hired, intending on going over his work and checking in on him. I liked to keep up with my employees and make sure they were settling in well when they joined the company. I never had to do that with an accountant before considering Artie was always with us, but that didn't really matter. Whatever role he was playing in the company, I wanted to make sure he felt comfortable and was a good fit. I was always in the belief that it was better to catch problems or inconsistencies early so they could be taken care of rather than letting them get worse and having to do damage control later. Besides, after the time we spent together the day he was hired, I already liked him and wanted to get to know him more.

Of course, that was before everything happened with his sister. Now it felt a bit on the awkward side to sit down across the desk from him and talk about how he was settling into the team. I decided not to use my usual line about wanting to keep things in the family. That was uncomfortable now, considering everything. And as I sat there listening to him talk about numbers and tell me anecdotes about his first week on the job, I couldn't help but wonder if he knew what had happened. It was obvious Merry and her brother were very close, so it wouldn't be completely out of the realm of expectation that she'd told him the story we came up with. Especially considering he was there the night we were caught kissing at the bar.

I'd already had that conversation with my brothers. They came over for our usual Sunday night time around the bonfire, and I made a point of pulling them aside so I could talk to them without my parents overhearing. Giving them a quick rundown of a made-up story was one thing. Telling my parents was something completely different. My brothers were guys, I justified. They'd been there before and knew what it was like to get wrapped up in a woman. Maybe they hadn't gone quite as far as I had. As far as I knew, none of them had ever had sex with a woman at work, especially a woman they weren't in a relationship with.

But as the oldest brother, I figured it was my job to set that precedent. Maybe.

I didn't really have any expectations for how they were going to react. The possibilities were spread far across the spectrum, so I just had to take each one as it came. Fortunately, it wasn't too bad. They weren't delighted with my impulsivity by a long shot, but it wasn't so much the sex in the office they were concerned about. Instead, it was who I'd chosen. Each of them went straight for the warnings, reminding me how good Merry was for the company and that everyone liked her. Even Vince and Nick liked her, and they had only encountered her briefly at the races. But they knew well enough to know she was good for the team and was doing fantastic work for the company. Losing her wasn't an option, according to all four.

Which was good, because I didn't want to lose her, either. I wanted to keep her. Except I was thinking about it in a different way than they were. While my brothers worried about her leaving the company, I was only thinking of how much I wanted to have her as a much closer part of my life. But that wasn't an option. Having her stay at the company was the most I could ask for, and that meant staying out of her way and not causing any more trouble.

The longer we talked, the more I thought Brandon seemed to have no clue what happened. He didn't look at me or speak to me any differently than he had before. And he definitely didn't mention it, which would have been so awkward I might not have been able to live through it. He just talked and updated like nothing was different, and finally the meeting was over.

It was a relief to close the door behind Brandon and be in my office alone for a while. It wasn't him. I liked talking to him and hoped eventually I'd be able to be in the room with him without immediately thinking of his sister. Right then, it was really anybody. I just wanted to be alone with my thoughts. I had press release stuff I needed to finish up and send to Merry to post; then I needed to respond to a slew of emails I'd put off for a couple days. After that, I was seriously considering spending the rest of the day in the garage. There was work to be done on the bikes, including two new ones we'd just bought. Getting my hands dirty might be just the thing I needed to help with the restless feeling under my skin.

Responding to the emails took longer than I expected. There was some interest from new sponsors, but I had to weed through the spam offers and strange attempts at creating partnerships to get to them. Merry had already told me I'd probably be hearing from people who would try to present themselves as internet celebrities or influencers who could get the company's name in front of their legion of followers. With sponsored posts, of course, and with the expectation of other perks and privileges to go along with it. Those aggravated me, both because of their arrogance and because they wasted my time.

Finally, I was finished with my emails and had nothing else to do that required me to be in the office. At least, nothing I couldn't comfortably leave until the next day. I was ready to go down to the garage and spend some time with my brother and father, blast music, and let my mind go for a while.

As soon as I walked into the kitchen to grab a bottle of water to bring with me outside, I knew I wasn't making it down to the garage unscathed. Standing at the counter over a pan of fresh cornbread was my mother. She turned on me, and the look on her face told me everything I needed to know.

She knew. I don't know how. I don't know who told her or what version they told her. But she knew.

"Hi, Mom," I said, trying to slip out the door.

She was too quick for me and cornered me.

"What's wrong with you?" she asked.

"What do you mean?"

"Did your father and I not teach you anything? Running a company is a tremendous responsibility. It's not just about making the right business decisions or choosing the right sponsorships. You have power when you run a company, and you have to respect that power and how it affects other people," she continued.

"Mom," I started, wanting to stop her where she was, but not getting very far.

"No. You're going to let me finish. There have been problems between you and Merry since the day she started working here, and I don't understand how we got here. A fling? Really Quentin? With an employee?"

"A fling that didn't go anywhere," I reminded her.

"Do you really think that makes a difference? If anything, that makes it worse," she said.

"How could that make it worse?" I asked.

"You slept with an employee, Quentin. You are in a position of power. That creates a dynamic that should never be taken advantage of. Especially if it's just something you're going to throw by the wayside because you didn't think it was going to go anywhere. That could be disastrous. She could quit, and nobody here wants that. I don't know what's going through your head or what you're doing to her head by toying with her like this, but you better figure it out. And do it fast before you lose her."

There was really nothing I could say. Arguing with her wouldn't do any good, and neither would trying to defend myself. I nodded and took my lecture, then left work, not even bothering to stop by the garage. Hearing my mother talk about 'losing' Merry had hit me in the gut in a way I didn't like. I knew she meant from a work standpoint, but my damn heart was already feeling something different.

28

MERRY

I needed a break. That might have been a tremendous understatement. I needed to get the hell out of the office and away from every person who was staring at me and all the questions they thought were fair game but were definitely not. As soon as I started working at the Freeman Racing complex, I felt the bond of the small group. Like Quentin had said, it was like a family, and there were major benefits to that. I felt welcomed and supported, I didn't have to worry about maintaining a strictly professional attitude all the time. I didn't have to wear pantyhose to work. That was one of my favorites. But now I knew the downside.

Apparently, the price of getting to work in the tight-knit environment meant being up for conversation whenever something interesting happened. That conversation quickly turned to gossip, and it burned through the complex so fast it would have devastated Smokey the Bear. And that was exactly what had happened with Quentin's and my fling. News of us hooking up spread through everybody who worked for the company so fast when I got to work, Glenda was already bubbling over with questions. It didn't seem to strike her as odd or inappropriate at all to try to glean every little detail out of me.

I wasn't sharing. They might have invited me into the grapevine, but I wasn't having any of it. The point of us saying we had a fling that didn't work out was to keep everybody from making too much of a big deal out of it. Clearly that didn't work out. We'd managed to start everybody chatting like old women in the hair salon, and by lunch I was just waiting for the complex to churn out their own tabloid just so we could be splashed on the cover.

It wasn't malicious. At least, it didn't feel that way. They weren't judging or criticizing, or even teasing. It was a lot of curiosity and intrigue, but it was too much. It had all gotten way too big, and I felt like I couldn't breathe. I needed air and I slipped out of the office to try to steal a few minutes to myself.

My favorite tree was appealing, but it was too out in the open. I didn't want to be sitting there and have someone else who hadn't already gotten their words in to stumble on me and decide I was open season because I was away from my office. Wanting to make sure I was as alone as possible, I headed further into the complex, toward the pond I'd seen on my first day. The thought of sitting there looking out over the water and enjoying some calm sounded amazing. Maybe I would even get to see the family of ducks that sometimes splashed around there.

As I went past the test track and approached the pond, though, I realized it was a bad idea. I wasn't going to be as alone as I wanted to be. But I didn't get the chance to change my mind and turn away. I was already caught.

Of course he was there. Of course Quentin would think to escape and go to the exact same place I'd thought of. And of course, he somehow sensed I was there and turned around before I could retreat.

He was sitting on a small bench close to the edge of the water, looking out over the pond just like I'd planned on doing. I paused when I saw him, wanting to backtrack and disappear back across the grounds. The last thing I needed right then was for somebody to see us out there in the secluded corner of the property and fuel even more murmurs about us. But I didn't get the chance. Before I could even take a step back, Quentin glanced back over his shoulder and saw me.

"Hey," he said. "Trying to hide out, too?"

I let out a short laugh. "Something like that."

He gestured to the empty spot beside him on the bench.

"Care to join me?" he asked. "We can hide out together."

Sighing, I walked over to the bench and sat down. At least I'd have someone to talk to that wasn't going to grill me for details about the 'fling.' He already knew the details. He was there for them. All of them.

"So, today has been fun," I said after a few seconds of silence.

"Something like that," he said.

"How's Darren?" I asked.

"Better," he told me.

We struggled through stilted small talk; the conversation made all the more awkward by my realization of my feelings for him. As much as I wanted to be alone when I got out of the office, and as unhappy as I was initially to see Quentin sitting on the bench, the longer I sat there, the more I realized I was glad he was there. Even with the strange tension and the awkwardness, having him close to me warmed me. The draw to him was stronger now, and no matter what was going on, I wanted him there.

Quentin shifted beside me, and I turned, thinking he might be getting up to leave. Instead, I saw his hand up, reaching out to touch my arm. Without a second thought, I slid across the bench toward him, sighing and melting into his touch.

Our lips met and we stayed there for a moment, basking in the touch of our mouths, the heat of each other's breath and taste of our tongues as they explored. I found myself grasping the sides of his face, pulling him into me, wanting to press myself into him, to feel his body mold around mine and know I was his and he was mine. I turned my body toward him, and his arm scooped around me, pulling me tightly against him. My breath rose and fell in hitches, the thrill of excitement and passion and taboo, being outside, just beyond the view of the complex, hidden by the small line of trees and the hill leading to the track.

A deep moan came from somewhere in his chest, and I melted into him. The sound of his voice, the hunger and desire in it, was like velvet, and I let it wrap around me, fill my ears with it and let it ring inside my head. I wanted that moan to be the only thing I heard for the rest of my life. It said so much without words. I opened my eyes and pulled back to take him in. His eyes burned into mine, and a rush of adrenaline filled me. I suddenly didn't give a fuck about anything but this moment, right here, right now. I could tell he felt it, too, and his hand slipped under my ass and pulled me onto his lap.

I straddled him, my dress flowing down over his legs, and I could feel the thick rod of his hard cock straining against the zipper of his pants. Our lips met again, and I ground my hips down, swiveling them and letting him brush against my core and feel how hot and wet my panties were. Another groan rumbled from his chest, and I caught it in my mouth, wanting to swallow it and let it fill my belly with his passion. His hands ran up my back, clutching at me, touching me everywhere his fingers would land, and then they dropped down to slide under my dress. Our tongues lashed at each other as his fingers dug into my ass, pulling me down into him so I could experience how hard he was for me. I felt like I was going to hyperventilate in my excitement and made myself breathe deeper.

Before I could try to move away and gather my bearings, one hand slid over my panties and touched me. All thought of trying to wiggle away left me, and I arched myself toward his touch. Fingers pulled aside the cotton, and his thumb pressed into my clit. He rotated it, circling around and teasing it open. I put a hand over my mouth to muffle a cry as a sudden, powerful orgasm rushed over me just at the touch of his fingers on me. I grasped the back of the bench to hold myself up as my body shook.

I needed him inside of me. As I came down off the wave of the powerful and surprisingly quick climax, I reached down between my legs to pull open his pants. Memories of my office when his cock was the only thing outside of his clothes thrilled me, no matter how much I wanted to strip him naked and lick every inch of his body. His zipper came down, and I unbuttoned his pants to get more access. He was long, and thick and throbbing with a need for my touch. I wrapped my fingers around it and stroked, enjoying the feeling of it pulsing in my grip. I looked back up into his eyes, and a grin spread across his face before his head leaned back to focus on the touch.

Pressing my knees down into the bench and sitting up on them, I guided the head of his cock to my opening and let it slide along the folds. He groaned as I pressed him into my clit and covered him with my wetness, making him slick and ready. I adjusted so the head was at my entrance and slowly slid down onto him. I couldn't help but cry out a little as he filled me, and his hand reached up to cup over my mouth. Something about him silencing me made it even hotter, and I groaned louder as I pushed down onto his cock. I waited as my pussy adjusted to his fullness, and a moan escaped me before I sat down completely and he pushed against my walls, bringing me pleasure in the pain of my stretching around him.

His hands cupped my ass and helped guide me into a rhythm on him. I scanned the top of the hill behind us to make sure we were still alone and was thankful for the distance from the track. I wasn't entirely sure I would have stopped even if I had seen someone. My need for him was all-encompassing. I rolled my hips, riding him and reveling in the feeling of him sliding out and then back deeper into my pussy. One arm wrapped around his neck, and he pulled down on the collar of my dress until one breast was exposed. Pushing away the cup of the bra, he latched his mouth around my nipple and suckled on me as I increased the speed.

My eyes were closed as I let him fill me and I focused on the ecstasy of his cock. I knew we didn't have long, not out here in the open, and I went faster, wanting to make him come as fast and hard as possible. I wanted to feel his body clench and shake and hear the roar of his climax in my ear like I had heard in my office. I was slamming onto him now, letting him guide me with his grip as he pulled me up and down, harder and faster. I was getting dizzy with stimulation and reached one hand down between my legs. I was close again, and I wanted him to feel the full measure of my orgasm on his cock. I wanted him to feel my body pulse and squeeze around him and let him know that his body created that ecstasy.

I touched my clit with one finger but felt it brushed away by his hand. A thumb pressed into me, and our lips crushed into one another again. I took control of the rhythm and made deeper, longer strokes, letting his hand rub my clit until I felt the powerful wave crashing over me again. My body locked up around him as I came, and I arched back, letting him take my breast into his mouth again as I climaxed hard.

I rocked a few more times, letting my body come down slowly from the orgasm, and looked into his eyes. There was still hunger there, and I wanted to please him. I wanted to feel his orgasm and know it was my body that gave it to him. I shuffled off him, letting his cock slide out of me, and settled beside him. He turned like he was going to face me, but I pushed him back. My hand reached down and clasped the base of his cock, and I kissed him deeply.

When our lips parted, I lowered my head into his lap. I had longed to take him into my mouth since I had seen his long thick cock the first time. Flicking my tongue over the head, I adjusted so that I could massage his balls underneath with one hand and stroke him into my mouth with the other. His moans above me told me that he was close already, and I slid him into my mouth as fully as I could take him. Tasting the juices of our combined bodies was sweet and sticky and warm, and I let my tongue ride down the underside of his cock, swirling as I rose back up toward the head.

I bobbed on him for a few moments, letting my hand stroke and twist with my mouth, my other hand gently but firmly massaging his orbs underneath. I felt one hand reach into my dress and wrap around my breast and the other fill with my hair. His groans were getting more desperate, faster. I knew he was about to climax, and I turned enough so that I could make eye contact again. His mouth was open as he prepared for his orgasm, and I let him guide me up and down.

He pulled me up, wrapping his fingers around my waist and pulling me back into his lap. He slid into me easily, and I rocked into his body again. He clasped my ass and pulled me, increasing my rhythm to a frenzied pace. It only took seconds before his body stiffened, and I clutched around him. My body responded with a third explosive climax as he exploded into me, and I milked him empty with my throbbing pussy. Finally, he relaxed, and I crumpled into him, letting him slide out of me.

29

QUENTIN

Just like the first time, as soon as we were done, reality seemed to hit both of us. It was like we got so completely wrapped up in each other and our primal need for one another, we forgot we existed in the real world we weren't the only ones there. But when we were done, it crashed in around us and we had to deal with the consequences. The first of which was awkwardness and embarrassment as we scrambled to make ourselves presentable again. The last time at least we were inside. It was her office, which was wrong on its own set of levels, but at least we weren't out in the open and potentially exposed to anybody who happened to come by. Now we were outside, and both of us rushed to smooth out our clothing and right ourselves.

I tried to look at Merry, to see what she might be thinking, but she wouldn't look me directly in the eye as she adjusted her clothes and put them back in place as fast as she could. When she was put together again, she looked at me. The expression in her eyes was something I didn't think I would ever be able to put behind me. I didn't even know what it was. Emotions and thought processes were hard to read, like a storm swirling within her. There had to be something I could say. I had to be able to diffuse the situation, but there was no chance. She brushed her hand back through her hair and looked over her shoulder across the complex.

"I have to get back," she said. "I didn't really expect to be gone this long, and there are some things I need to do."

"Merry," I said, taking a step toward her. "We can't just walk away from each other."

"I'm sorry. I'm expecting a call, and I really don't want to miss it," she said.

It was a weak excuse, completely nonsensical in the situation. But it was obvious she was searching for anything she could find to disengage herself from the circumstances, from me. She was so uncomfortable she wanted to get away from me as fast as she possibly could and would use any excuse that popped into her mind. Before I could say anything else to her, she turned and hurried away. I stood there by the bench, trying to wrap my head around what just happened.

How could I let that happen? How could I do it again? After everything I'd thought through, all the conversations, all the guilty feelings. After struggling through conversations with her and forcing myself to accept there couldn't be anything between us because it was just too much. And yet somehow, I had so little thought and control I ended up right there all over again. Only this time, it was worse. Much worse.

I wanted her. That wasn't even a question. I'd come to accept that and figured it was just going to be something that existed somewhere in the back of my mind until it fizzled out. Or it wouldn't, and I'd just have to deal with it for as long as we worked together. Either way, wanting her and actually going after her were two different things. I definitely wanted to have her again, but outside on a bench? At work... again? How was it possible I could lose so much control over myself and my own responsibility that I let myself do that? What made it worse was that look in her eyes. The way she looked at me as she hastily got dressed and right before she ran off. It told me this wasn't something we'd be able to just brush off again.

By the time I got back home, I kind of wanted to kick my own ass. That about summed up how I was feeling about myself and my decision making. If I knew anyone else who slept with their much-younger employee not only once, but twice, and after they talked through it and knew it was a bad thing, my first thought would be to smack some sense into them. It only seemed appropriate now. Unfortunately, that wasn't going to have the effect I was going for, and no matter how much I tried to convince him, Cole just wasn't into the idea of doing me a solid and giving me a nice square kick in the ass. His explanation had something to do with us being grown men and the time he spent in Tibet, but I didn't care. I felt like shit and just wanted it to be over.

I got in the shower and stood under the water that was so hot it stung my skin. Turning the showerhead to a pulse setting, I hung my head down and let the streams pound down onto my neck and shoulders to try to loosen the muscles up. It felt like they were all tied in knots, and I couldn't get them to relax. The water helped, not just in tenderizing me like a steak, but also in filling my head with sound so I could ignore all the thoughts rushing through it for a little while.

When the water ran cold, I got out and stood in front of the foggy mirror. As the fog cleared and I was able to look at my reflection, I considered it carefully. I was never one of those people to spend much time staring into mirrors and contemplating myself. A quick glance at my reflection in the morning to confirm my clothes went together and my hair was straight was all I needed to get me through the day. But that evening, I forced myself to stand there and have a long, hard think session about what I was seeing.

There I was. Over forty. Perpetually single. Making mistakes right and left with a woman I could actually see myself with but who I had managed to completely screw up any chances with. It wasn't the best evaluation. But it was accurate. That's who I was, but it's not who I wanted to be. I just didn't know how to fix it. Any of it. Especially with Merry. We'd barely fixed it the last time.

I walked away from the mirror and put on boxers. It was still early in the evening, but I wasn't feeling up to doing much. After an in-depth tour of my kitchen where I came to the conclusion my full cabinets and refrigerator offered me nothing worth eating for the night, I wished I'd thought to swing by the kitchen before leaving the complex and grab something Mom baked. She was in a daily bake-a-thon habit now, and everybody at work was bringing home the spoils. I'd been so thrown off by the encounter with Merry it didn't even cross my mind.

But even if I had, I probably wouldn't have wanted to eat it. Nothing sounded good right then. It was like all my pleasure sensors had shut down and now nothing was going to be enjoyable anymore. I probably deserved that. It was some sort of cosmic justice for taking way too much pleasure where I shouldn't have.

I finally settled on giving up and ordering pizza. I brought it into the living room and lounged in my recliner, the box in my lap and a beer open beside me. After several slices and my second beer, I wasn't feeling much better, but

I also wasn't feeling worse, which I was going to take as a victory. It wasn't until I was most of the way through my third gory action movie that I admitted to myself I was checking my phone every few minutes to see if Merry had gotten in touch with me.

She hadn't, of course. She made it clear as soon as she scurried away and left me alone on that bench, she was determined to not acknowledge what happened and just go back to work. I felt fairly certain she was doing everything she could to try to convince her brain it didn't happen. Maybe she could get back to her office having replaced the memories with just sitting placidly by the pond by herself. I knew she wasn't going to reach out to me, so I had to decide how I was going to handle the situation and what I was going to do next. I could let it drop. Just go to work the next day like nothing, keep up with the story spreading around the complex, and try not to think about it anymore.

Or I could try to talk to her. At least let her know I was open to having a conversation if she was. It was possible she just didn't want to be the one to broach the subject. I thought about this through the end of the movie, then headed to bed. I reached for my phone as I got under the covers and sent off a fast text to her.

Do we need to talk?

I moved to set my phone back down on the nightstand, figuring I probably wouldn't hear back from her until the next morning. But before my hand even left the phone, it alerted to a return message from her.

No.

That was it. Just a simple "no." It seemed nothing if not final, and that only made me hate myself even more.

30

MERRY

Somehow despite all my promises to myself, all my contemplation about what happened and resolutions in my mind that I was enough of an adult to handle whatever feelings were happening inside me, it had happened again. I had made another mistake. Only this time, it was exponentially worse. Worse because I should have learned from the first time I made it. And worse because of how it happened. Sex outside, in the middle of the day, on work property. Not even in the privacy of an office. Just right out in the open next to the pond where anybody could have stumbled on us at any second. It wasn't just embarrassing because of what we were doing, but because of what it said about us. About me. What kind of woman had that little control over herself? What kind of woman couldn't deal with inconvenient attraction the way a normal adult does, but shoving it down and pretending it wasn't there?

Or maybe that's not the way a normal adult would handle it at all, because people didn't end up forming feelings for their bosses and then giving in to them. I didn't even recognize myself when I got home that night. Quentin probably thought I'd gone right back to work as soon as we were done. I wouldn't really expect him to think anything less, considering that's what I told him I was doing before hurrying away. In reality, I went right to the parking lot and I drove home. I called Brandon when I got back to the apartment and told him I would pick him up after work, but he could tell something was wrong and said he would just get a rideshare. I spent the rest of the day curled up on my living room couch, contemplating how I managed to get to this place.

Several times throughout the day, I reached for my phone, thinking about whether or not I should contact Quentin. On the other hand, I had no idea what I would say to him if I did. I didn't even know what I was thinking or feeling, so how could I possibly express it to him? That was a conversation I didn't want to face, especially not now. So, when I got a text from him that night asking if we needed to talk, I simply told him no. He didn't push, didn't insist. Finally, I felt like we could drop it.

Unfortunately for me and my state of mind, not everybody shared that sentiment. I dug my heels in, more committed than ever to making sure I was doing a good job and being a benefit to the company. Quentin had been extremely clear when he told me there were no rules against fraternization and my job wasn't at risk, but I'd been in the professional sphere long enough to know just because there wasn't a rule against something didn't mean you should just go ahead and do it. I didn't want to look like I was slacking off or becoming complacent. I didn't want it to fuel any rumors around the complex that I was a boss's pet and getting extra perks on the job because of some relationship with him. So, I tucked my head down and dedicated myself to work. I was polite to everyone to a fault, got to work early and left late, worked harder than I ever had. And very purposely avoided working with Quentin alone at any time.

But Minnie wasn't having any of the pretending. As far as I was concerned, no mention of any relationship between Quentin and I needed to see the light of day ever again. She didn't agree. Just a week after Quentin and I had sex again, she came to my office to talk. At first, she said it was just to check in. But considering in all the time I'd worked at the company she hadn't stopped by my office at all and instead had relied on me coming to her, I knew it wasn't just to make sure we were still building up our Twitter followers. She wanted to check in with me about Quentin and the stories she'd heard.

"Hey, Merry," she said. "How are you doing?"

"Fine," I told her. "Things are going well."

"With everything?" she asked.

"All the platforms, yes," I told her. "Visits to all of the accounts are up, and we are seeing a steady increase in all forms of engagement from leaving comments to reposting content."

"What about other things?" she asked.

I looked at her as if I didn't know what she was talking about, hoping it may make her uncomfortable enough for her to drop the conversation.

"What other things?" I asked.

The innocent look didn't work.

"Things other than work. You seemed a little distracted over the last week. And I've noticed you haven't been socializing with anybody like you were before. Especially Quentin. I thought the two of you had planned on having regular meetings to discuss your social media campaign," she said.

"We did," I said. "But since things have been going well, we've decided email works just as well."

Minnie nodded politely but I knew she didn't buy one bit of my story. She was way too shrewd of a woman not to know the real reason things had changed between Quentin and me. Without saying anything or telling me what she was doing, in the coming days she made efforts to help me work around being near Quentin. It felt good to be so appreciated and valued that she did not immediately side with her son and instead did what she could to create harmony in the office. I hoped it wouldn't last for too long and soon it would just fade into memory so everything could go back to normal.

That conversation had been nearly a month ago, and things were still tense around the office. It was only made worse by the bug I'd picked up at some point over the last week. Usually I was a very healthy person and managed to skate by the annual cold and flu season without falling victim. I might spend a day sneezing and coughing, but it had been years since the last time I'd felt truly ill for more than twenty-four hours. But this thing was sticking. I didn't have a fever, but I didn't have as much energy as usual, and everything I ate made me want to throw up. I tried to think about everybody I'd been in contact with, but no one I knew of was dealing with the stomach flu. I must have picked it up somewhere without realizing it. I made a mental note to start using those disinfecting wipes grocery stores put next to the carts.

I did my best to push through it and not let being under the weather keep me from fulfilling my responsibilities. After a few days of feeling sick, though, I knew it wasn't just going to go away. Maybe some extra rest would help. Minnie was understanding when I called in sick, and

Brandon transformed the living room of our apartment into a sick bay for me. He brought me soup and juice, reminding me regularly it didn't matter if I felt sick, I had to stay hydrated. Taking a few sips every now and then seemed to help settle my stomach. Except for the orange juice. That definitely made it worse.

He was a fantastic nurse for almost two days before I told him he needed to get out and have some fun. It wasn't just about me feeling sick or him taking care of me. After all, it wasn't like he had to do a whole lot. I barely wanted to eat and spent most of my time sleeping and watching TV. Instead, it was about how attached he had become to the apartment and the routine of just going to work and coming back. I didn't want him to fall into a habit of not doing anything or seeing anyone, so I encouraged him to call up some friends and go out to dinner. My single request was that he not bring back any leftovers. I didn't want the smell to make me feel any worse than I already did.

It wasn't long after he left before Olivia showed up at the apartment. She let herself in using the extra key I gave her for emergencies. I groaned when I saw her.

"Did Brandon call you?" I asked.

"Yes, he did," she said. "Somebody had to. You didn't even tell me you were sick."

"That's because I'm not sick," I told her. "I'm just not feeling great. I think I'll probably just worked myself too hard and I'm exhausted."

"All right. Well, what are your symptoms?" she asked.

"I'm tired. And I feel sick to my stomach. Not like all the time, but it lasts for a while when I do," I told her.

"Not all the time?" she asked. "What do you mean?"

"I only really start to feel like I'm going to throw up

after I eat. Sometimes I'm a little woozy, but if I smell food or attempt to eat anything solid, it gets really bad."

She stared at me, not blinking for a few seconds.

"How long is this been going on?" she asked.

"About a week," I told her. "That's why I decided to take some time off. I thought maybe if I got some rest, it would make it feel better."

"So, let me get this straight. You are tired. Smells bother you. And you feel sick when you eat. But you haven't had a fever or coughing or sneezing? Anything like that?"

"No," I told her.

"And you haven't gone to a doctor?" she asked.

"No. Why would I go to a doctor? I told you, I'm not sick," I said.

"I think you're probably right about that. But you still need to go to at least go to the drugstore," Olivia told me.

"Why would I do that?" I asked.

"To get a pregnancy test. That sounds exactly like how my sister felt when she was pregnant with my nephew," she said matter-of-factly.

Panic started bubbling up inside me as I tried to flip through the calendar, timing my encounters with Quentin. It hadn't even occurred to me that I'd missed my period. With all the stress and chaos going on around me, it hadn't even crossed my mind. And of course, we hadn't used a condom either time. It wasn't like I walked around carrying a stash of them. Reality sunk in hard, and I rushed to get dressed. I didn't care how dizzy or tired I felt after two days of barely eating. I needed to get to the drugstore and fast. We were back at the apartment within half an hour, and Olivia sat on the floor of the hallway just outside the bathroom door while I took the test.

"Starting the timer," I called out when I finished peeing on the stick.

"I'm going to make you some dry toast. Barely any smell. Barely any taste. Maybe you'll be able to keep it down," Olivia told me.

By the time she was back to the hallway carrying the plate, I was standing in the doorway of the bathroom with the stick in my hand. She met my eyes, and I fell into her arms crying.

31

QUENTIN

I watched Merry walk down the hallway past my office again, and I swore her footsteps got faster when she got near my door. Her shoes clicked loudly against the floor. Her pace would be steady and casual as she started her way down the hall, then get quicker and shorter as she made her way past my office, then slow again as she continued away from my door. It wasn't enough to consider it a full-out run or anything, but she was not wasting time getting away from my orbit.

If it was anyone else, I would think the rushing was only because it was race day and everybody on the complex was busting their butts to try to get ready for the big event that night. The tailgate party at the last race was a massive success. People had started emailing and messaging by the next day asking if we were having another one and if they had to buy tickets for it. It was exciting, but it only meant a mountain more work preparing for the night's race, and I wouldn't think twice about anyone else even full sprinting past my office. If nothing more than to look like they were working their hardest.

But I knew Merry was scurrying past me for another reason. She didn't want me to notice she was there so I wouldn't try to talk to her. Or even if I did notice her, she wanted to be moving too fast for me to get up and come after her. Not that the thought hadn't crossed my mind several times already that day. I wanted to talk to her more than anything else. The first time I saw her walk by the office, I moved to get up, wanting to go find her and bring her into a quiet room so I could just get a few minutes with her. But I stopped myself before I even made it around to the front of my desk. I knew I wasn't supposed to do that. I wasn't supposed to try to find any time alone with her or have any conversations about anything but work.

Hell, I wasn't even supposed to want those things. All my thoughts and concentration were supposed to be on nothing but doing what I was supposed to be doing to fulfill my role in the company. And that role was to do my own damn job, to keep the company afloat, and keep our team winning. That was it. Those were supposed to be my only goals, and I had to stay laser-focused to make sure they did. Staying focused meant staying away from her. And I certainly wasn't the only one paying attention to my actions and making sure I was on my best behavior. Nobody was saying anything to me about it, of course, but I couldn't help but notice the way everybody was looking at me and how they reacted every time I so much as shifted my weight if she was mentioned or was walking past the office.

It was ridiculous, really. The whole damn company had taken her side. These people were practically my family, and I'd known them most of my life. Some of them actually *were* my family. The point was, as much as I knew why they were doing it, it seriously sucked to have everybody standing up for her almost like they were making some sort of wall around her with their thoughts and pressures.

But then again, it was exactly the way it should be. In all honesty, this was what I'd created for myself. I was the cad who couldn't keep my hands off my pretty young employee and had let my attraction to her get the best of me. Not once, but twice. But at least everybody only sort of knew about that first time. Even with only that, I deserved the way everyone was reacting to me. At least it wasn't all negative. Some were giving me the cold shoulder, but others, mostly my family, were giving me looks. They were hard to describe because they changed so much. Sometimes they were sad. Sometimes they were a little angry. Sometimes they were just flat-out judgmental, but they were going to keep it in because I was family and they didn't want to hurt me. That was a special kind of look. One of those facial expressions only people from the South really understand. It's part of our culture right up there with the sweet tea and salted watermelon at picnics.

I dragged my hand back through my hair. It was getting long. I hadn't noticed, but now I realized in the last several weeks I'd been too distracted to bother making an appointment at the barber. That was just another sign of how distracted and disconnected I'd become recently. Usually I looked forward to my haircuts. They were a time to relax a bit and catch up with the same barber who had been cutting my hair for the last twenty years. But I had managed to miss at least two appointments and was definitely seeing the effects. I was going to have to make a point to call James the next day and make an appointment. Maybe I would even have a hot shave. it would probably do me good after all the tension I'd been dealing with.

I tried to focus on the work in front of me again, but that

telltale click of shoes started coming down the hallway again. This time I didn't let myself look up to watch her hurry past. Maybe if she glanced in and saw I was still looking at my desk rather than up at her it would take the edge off a bit. Everybody around the complex was taking their cues from her. As long as Merry was uncomfortable and acting like something was off, everybody else would, too. I looked forward to when this would finally blow over and we could get back to normal.

Only I wasn't sure when that would ever happen. The feelings definitely weren't gone, and I didn't see any difference coming on the horizon. She'd gotten under my skin, and no matter how much I told myself it wasn't what was good for either one of us, it didn't matter. This was what I was living with now. But maybe there was a chance I could ignore it or swallow it down. I could force myself to act like everything was normal, and that would put everything right again.

As soon as she passed by, I got up and headed out of the office. There was really no point in me trying to do any office-type work that day. My brain was in a totally different place, and it wasn't going to do any good. All I could do was go down to the garage and check in with Darren and Greg. We had a race that night, and I wanted to see how the team was doing.

The first race back after his crash and poor showing had been nerve-racking for Darren. He was nervous all the way up to the day of the race, practicing late into the night and taking his poor bike apart at least three times. But a third-place showing got some of his confidence back, and the next race he won first again. Greg came in second both of those times, and it was obvious he was gunning for first. He'd gotten his taste of what it was like to be on top and now wanted more.

But it was good to see both riders were still acting like they were on the same team. Rather than there being fierce, unpleasant competition between the two of them, they played off each other and used one another as motivation. Both wanted to do the best they could, but they genuinely wanted the other to do well, too. It was good to see, and I knew it made for a stronger team and an even more successful company.

When I got down to the garage, Dad was talking to Darren and Greg. His hands were up over his head and his face was high with color, telling me he was in the midst of one of his famous stories about the early days of the company. By the way he told the stories it sounded like he ran a racing company in the Wild West and that any second there could have been a shootout in the middle of the track. But it was always fun to listen to him, and I leaned against the frame of the bay door to hear the end of the story.

"That's one of my favorites," I said when he was finished.

Dad turned to me with a broad grin.

"I guess you've heard it a time or two," he said.

"At most," I joked, but the jubilant sound I intended for my voice fell flat.

"I guess we should be getting back to work," he said.

"What are you working on?" I asked.

Dad and Darren exchanged glances. There was something in that look, but I wasn't sure what it was. Dad gestured to the bikes in front of him.

"We're just doing some last-minute checks and adjustments," he said. "We want to make sure we're ready for tonight."

"That's a good idea," I told them. "The other teams are going to be coming for us after we've done so well the last few races. We want to make sure we stay on top."

"And make sure we don't let anyone that get us in another crash," Greg pointed out.

"Also important to keep in mind," I said.

They went back to their work, and I did my best to pay attention and be useful, but I quickly realized why my brother and father were looking suspiciously at each other. I was just about useless. It was like everything I ever knew about the bikes and racing had leaked out of my head and I wasn't able to understand anything that was going on. The words just went through me, and I had nothing beneficial to add to the conversation. Finally, I stopped trying. I stepped back from what was going on and just watched. At least I wasn't sitting in the office waiting for the sound of her shoes anymore.

As he walked around to the other end of the bikes, Darren came up beside me and clamped a hand on my shoulder. I looked at him, and he grinned. He didn't say anything, but I got what he meant by it. It was a lot coming from Darren, and I appreciated it. As fun and silly as my youngest brother could be, he sometimes struggled with difficult emotions. He hated to see anybody upset and often didn't know how he was supposed to react. He was firmly on Merry's side in this situation but wanted to make sure I knew he was still my brother and would always be there for me.

It was finally time to leave for the race. This time we were all leaving together to make sure the team was available for the tailgate event. Because we showed up for only part of the first one, many of the comments we got through our social media channels about the party were saying the fans wanted to see more of us. Requests for pictures and autographs were frequent, and several people even said they loved the idea of us grabbing some food and hanging out with them for a while. I made them feel like we were friends. I looked forward to trying to relax and have fun, to remind myself of the importance of the fans and why we worked so hard.

But I couldn't help but be distracted knowing a few cars behind me in the caravan was Merry and her brother, and I wouldn't be able to escape being near her tonight.

32

MERRY

I couldn't help but be proud of the success of the tailgate event. It was one of those things I never really envisioned myself doing. Especially not with the career path I'd chosen. As a social media consultant, it was my responsibility to evaluate and maintain social media presence for companies. It was all about creating effective social media platforms, maintaining engagement with customers and fans, and trying to build up more visibility so the companies could enjoy the benefits of a world that was increasingly virtual. And yet when I started working with Freeman Racing, my idea of my work responsibilities completely shifted. All of a sudden, I cared more about the company and the people who worked for it than I ever had about any other client. It wasn't just about making sure their social media was at its best. Of course, that was at the forefront of what I was doing, but I was constantly thinking of as many other ways as I could to boost the company and bring them into a new era.

Thinking of it that way felt a little bit arrogant. Like I was going to be their Fairy Godmother who could just swoop in and suddenly make everything better. It almost felt like I was suggesting they didn't know how to run their own company and weren't successful. But that's not what I meant. They were already successful and popular, but there were ways it could get better. I was under the firm belief that there are always ways companies could improve and reach higher levels of success. No matter how beloved they were among the populace, no matter how much money they were making or how well they performed in the market, there was always something they could do better. There were ways they could be stronger.

And even though I came into this without any knowledge about racing and no idea how a racing fan thought, I quickly grew attached and found myself wanting to do more. Fortunately, they were extremely supportive of me. Minnie especially. She was always interested to hear my ideas and work with me to polish them up into workable plans. That's how it was with these parties. It all started with us chatting about nothing in particular and me ending up sharing a story from my high school days. I was telling her about homecoming and the tailgating party one of the student organizations put together. It was so much fun and one of my favorite memories.

From there, I threw out the idea of using that model to build up fan engagement and get the team connected with the people who came out race after race watch them. The first one was a gamble. Nobody was really sure if anybody would want to come and if they would be interested in sticking around or buying merchandise. But it was wildly successful, and we ended up completely selling out of the shirts we had for sale and giving away all the other pieces of swag we'd ordered.

Even after that success, I was possibly even more

nervous about the second one. I wondered if the novelty of it had drawn in the first crowds and that time it wouldn't be interesting anymore, so the attendance would dwindle. Instead, it was just as busy if not more. From there, it was just a part of the race we looked forward to.

Last night's had been probably the best. The team agreed to be more of a part of it rather than just stopping by, and fans were lined up to take pictures with Darren and Greg. We hired two more food trucks to offer more variety, and the merchandise table was cleared out well before the event started. Halfway through, Gus came running up to me, his eyes bright and filled with excitement as he told me he wanted to bring one of the old bikes that wasn't being used in races anymore but was still in good condition. They were sometimes used as decoration around the complex or at shows, so he thought it would be fun to bring one to a party so fans could sit on it for pictures.

It was great to see everybody so excited and involved. The only challenge I had was staying away from the beer. The first couple of parties I enjoyed a beer while I was eating. I knew I was technically at work, but everyone else in the family tipped one back, and Minnie reassured me it was just fine. So, this time she offered to get me one when we first arrived. She didn't seem to think anything strange about the first time I declined, but she offered more throughout the evening and looked at me with more questions in her eyes every time. It was a departure from the norm, and she definitely noticed.

But I got through the party with no beer and no direct questions. The race went well, and a photo finish of Darren and Greg all but tying for first well ahead of the rest of the pack earned the rest of the week off work for everyone. They went back to the complex after the race to unload and put everything away, but then the complex would be closed until Monday morning.

Which was exactly why I was there first thing in the morning Friday. I gave myself Thursday to sleep in and relax, giving in to the tiredness that seemed to never really go away now that I was sharing my body with a whole other human being. But Friday I decided to take advantage of the complex being closed and headed into the office. Everybody being gone meant I could just work casually and catch up on some of the analytical stuff I'd missed when I was out sick for those two days.

I still wasn't feeling at my absolute best. What people called morning sickness didn't just strike in the morning. It tended to linger with me mostly in the afternoon and sometimes when I very first woke up. Managing it had become somewhat paradoxical. Now that I knew I wasn't actually ill and instead was just coping with pregnancy symptoms, I had to find ways to deal with them and still be able to function every day. But that meant eating lunch and sometimes dinner would inevitably make me feel sick to my stomach, but if I didn't eat crackers before I even put my feet on the floor when I woke up in the morning, I was likely to feel sick, too. I also realized eating snacks throughout the morning would help to calm everything down, and sometimes I was able to get a small meal in later in the day. I learned to subsist on protein shakes to get in enough nutrition, and I hoped this stage would be over soon.

Olivia was still the only person in my life who knew, and I honestly still had no idea what I was going to do about it. It was such a strange concept, something I never expected and never really thought about. I didn't know what to think about it, much less how to handle it. I couldn't decide if I should tell Quentin. Though if I were to listen to

Olivia, that wasn't even an option. She was very clear in her belief that I had to tell him. It wasn't up to me to decide if he should know or not. This was as much his baby as it was mine, and he had the right to make his decision about how he felt about it just as much as I did.

That was a lot to think about. Not just if to tell him, but how to tell him, and how I was going to cope with however he reacted. After all, I wasn't going to be able to keep it a secret for too much longer, and unless I wanted to quit my job before I started showing, I needed to figure my shit out.

At least being at the complex alone meant I didn't have to try to impress anybody with what I was wearing or look even close to professional. I could just relax and do what I needed to do at my own pace. It was a blisteringly hot day, so I chose shorts and a tank top. No one else was around, so I turned my music on and had it blasting to keep me company and keep my energy up. I was lost in the rhythm of one of my favorite songs and the pattern of checking analytics when a knock scared me. Jumping back, I looked up at the door and saw Quentin standing there. His hand was still hovered over where he leaned in to knock on the open door. I immediately noticed he didn't look like I was used to. Rather than his suit or slacks and button-up, he was wearing shorts and an old college T-shirt. It was charming to see him that way, looking like just a normal person who could kick back and have fun without having to think about work.

The irony wasn't lost on me that I was seeing him look that way while he was in fact at work. But at least now I knew he owned those clothes, which meant that was a possibility of another side of him I didn't know. Even when we were at the bar celebrating my brother getting his new position, he'd been in his business clothes and carried himself with a certain degree of tension. The only time he let go was when we were kissing. And when we were on my desk. And when we were on the bench at the side of the pond.

Which brought me to this awkward moment as I stood staring at him, wondering if he could sense something different about me. Was that even possible? Maybe that was a bit on the far side, but the way he was looking at me made me wonder. There was a look in his eyes I didn't really know how to interpret. There was no way he could see anything yet. I was only a few weeks along, so nothing was different. But he was looking at me with some sort of expectation.

Finally, Quentin mumbled an apology and a string of other words I didn't quite catch. Something about not knowing anyone else was here and wondering where the music was coming from. He rushed away down the hall before I had a chance to say anything back. I stood there and stared at the empty doorframe for a while, wondering what that interaction was all about. He hadn't interacted with me directly in weeks, not even at the tailgate event. I'd made it a point to not be alone with him at any time and did my best to avoid getting near him at all. And yet he showed up at my office and stared at me like he was waiting for something.

Whether there was any chance of him knowing something was going on or not, I needed to figure out my next move. I tried to turn my focus back to work, but it was hard to get myself back into it again. My mind had wandered to the baby and what I was supposed to do. The reality was hovering over me that I needed to make a decision soon. The longer I put off my plan, the harder it was going to be to deal with it. I needed to come up with something before I started showing.

33

QUENTIN

I was grateful to have a full house that week. While it was important for me to take the time off away from everybody so I could think about what was going on in my life and how I was going to handle it, the solitude wasn't an option for me. I needed to be around the people I was closest to, people who loved me no matter what. Even if they were upset with me and didn't think I was making good decisions in my life, they were still the ones I relied on and trusted the most.

In fact, it was when I was on the wrong path and making decisions that weren't good for me that I needed them the most. Not just to direct me and tell me what they thought I should be doing. Not to admonish me to make sure I knew I was doing something wrong. Those were things I was more than capable of doing by myself and didn't need any help with. Instead, I needed them around me so I could know that no matter what, I still had that support system. But even when I was spiraling out of control until nothing else in my life was falling into place, I had them. My family, including Cole, was my rock, and my security. They reassured me and reminded me of the type of person I wanted to be.

Seeing my parents together was always a refreshing boost for my spirits. When I was feeling down or helpless about life, when I was discouraged and felt like there was nothing good to come of any type of relationship, I looked to them. Their love was still strong after almost fifty years of marriage. In fact, it almost seemed like being together kept them young. Their laughter and joy at one another belied their years, and I knew if either of them ever had to be without the other one, it would quickly make them wither away.

That was something I'd never experienced. But seeing it in them gave me some sort of hope. More important than that, seeing them together and having my brothers around kept my mind active and stopped me from wallowing and being sad. It didn't really take away the emptiness or the sadness dragging down on my heart, but it made it so I didn't have to think about it all the time.

There was loud yelling in my backyard, this time punctuated by excited, high-pitched barks. Many times over the years since I'd bought this house and transformed it into my own custom home, I felt gratitude for being on so much land and not near my neighbors. While there was a certain appeal to being able to walk over to a neighbor's house and get a cup of sugar or have a conversation on the porch, that was outweighed by the potential disruption and aggravation caused by the sheer volume achieved by my family. I would just have to make sure my pantry stayed properly stocked with sugar and be satisfied with the conversations I could have with my brothers.

The more the puppy barked and yipped, the more my brothers laughed and cheered. As usual, I was inside the kitchen putting together snacks and gathering drinks. It seemed that no matter how much I prepared for these gatherings and thought I had brought enough down to my outdoor kitchen, inevitably I ran out of food or beverages partway through the fire. But that was fine. Going back up to the main house gave me a few minutes to myself to let my mind clear and my ears stop ringing. Carrying everything in a huge bucket with a large tray balanced over the top, I headed back out onto the deck. My father looked up and noticed me trying to negotiate making it down the steps carrying everything.

He immediately hopped up and came to help me. We made it down to the grass, and I watched my brothers running around playing keep-away with the new puppy and Cole. It looked like we were little children again, and I couldn't help feeling the urge to jump in. The puppy was growing fast, and it was so much fun to watch her run and jump, flopping around in the grass and delightedly climbing on the logs and benches. We didn't bother to light the fire that night because it was so hot, so I didn't feel worried about her safety. I was enjoying seeing her be so free and full of life.

Having a pet wasn't something I'd ever thought about. Working so much wasn't exactly conducive to being at home and seeing to the needs of an animal. Up until fairly recently when I forced myself to start cooking more for myself, I could barely keep myself fed and would often forget things like bringing my clothes to the dry cleaner or starting the dishwasher. For as much control and organization I had in the office, my personal life was often a mess. I didn't want to entrust myself with the life of another living creature. But seeing this little one bounce around might have been changing my mind.

It surprised the hell out of me I was actually considering getting myself a dog. But the more I watched her, the more I thought maybe it would help the loneliness that had taken over my heart. It was hard to admit that, but I could. I had gotten to that place now that I really could admit it. I was lonely. And it was my own damn fault. I went about pursuing my attraction to Merry exactly the wrong way and lost out on any chance of actually trying to have an honest relationship with her. Close bonds and love like my parents had between them didn't come from two illicit sexual encounters at work. That type of thing made really being together impossible. So, my coping mechanism at that point was doing the only thing that made sense to do.

I was drinking my feelings.

I sat in one of the lounge chairs and took down what I wanted to say with my third beer but could possibly be much further down the line than that. I'd stopped really counting. It wasn't the most responsible choice in the world, but I wasn't batting a thousand with my decision-making skills recently, so I wasn't going to worry about it so much. A few minutes later, Dad came up to me.

"Is there anything else I have in the house we need to get?" he asked.

"No," I told him. "We got everything."

"Do you want to go check?" he asked.

I knew that was code. It meant *get up and come with me because we need to have a talk.* That was a departure from the normal. Usually it was my mother who cornered me for a heart-to-heart talk. Or a good tongue-lashing when she felt I needed it. But this time it was my father who was stepping in to try to drag my out-of-control train to a stop. Finishing off the rest of the beer, I followed him up the steps onto my back deck. I tossed the bottle into the recycling bin and dropped down onto the swinging glider in one corner. Dad sat down beside me, and for a few seconds we just swung back and forth in silence.

Finally, he tilted his head slightly toward me.

"You know, your mom kicked me to the curb for a solid year," he said.

"Wait, what? When?"

"Oh a long time ago now."

"What did you do?" I asked.

"I crawled my way back to her," he said. "It took me that long to get over myself and realized what needed to be done. I did it, though, and it's been the two of us ever since. I can't imagine anyone else in my life. That woman is my life, and I would do it all over again in a heartbeat, but if I had to I do it all again, I would go back to her the next day. Pride and feeling too manly and powerful be damned. When it's worth it, it's worth groveling for."

He got up after that and walked away. It was a very short heart to heart, but it made a major impact on me. I had no idea that had happened between my parents. All that mattered was my dad messed up in some way and my mother kicked him out of her life, then held her ground while she waited for him to realize what he did.

It took him humbling himself and being able to admit he wasn't always right, that he not only did something wrong, that he absolutely needed her. That was probably the hardest part. Admitting to being wrong wasn't usually that much of a challenge. Especially not when you had three brothers who were more than willing to step up and show you all the ways that you were wrong. What was harder was admitting my fear that there was a place in my heart that was so open to Merry. I didn't want there to be. I didn't want there to be a place open for anybody. It was too much vulnerability, too much possibility of being hurt again.

But, actually, I *did* want it to be there for her. More than I could have ever imagined I wanted it. The conversation left me wondering just how much my family really knew about what happened between Merry and me. Obviously, they knew we'd had a fling. That's what we told them. But it seemed they could sense something else. I wondered how much they could see, and even more than that, if she could see it too. If there was ever a chance she might be able to forgive me.

The chances didn't seem great. She all but hid behind people at the tailgate party in her efforts not to be within a few feet of me, and when I ran into her at the office unexpectedly, she just stared at me without a word. Of course, I didn't say anything to her, either. I couldn't. The music blaring caught my attention, and I went in search of the computer or radio someone had obviously left playing when we headed to the race. But then I discovered it wasn't something someone left on by accident. It was Merry, hanging out in her office and humming to the music as she swayed back and forth, staring at the tablet in her hands.

I'd seen her look at her tablet, checking over things and adding to the platforms, countless times by then. But it was different seeing her do it with the music streaming around the office and her wearing nothing but little shorts and a tank top. It was like seeing a completely different side of her, a glimpse into a more real version of her that few probably got to enjoy. I wanted to say something to her. Anything. But I knew if I stepped even one foot into that office or she got any closer to me, I wasn't going to be able to control my actions. I couldn't let that happen again.

34

MERRY

The complex went back to normal on Monday, and everything was business as usual by Tuesday. I'd finally been working on the social media platforms long enough that real data was coming in. Sometimes it was difficult to explain that to businesses when I first started working for them. They wanted to see immediate and astonishing results they could easily measure. They seemed to think a couple of tweets and a blog post or two would instantly transform their visibility and make them more appealing. While that was possible, they really couldn't expect everything to go viral and become the next internet sensation.

It really didn't work that way most of the time. Of course, if it was a brand-new company that never had any social media presence before, the difference between nothing and how they would interact when things got up and going was noticeable. And if something caught on exceptionally well, there could definitely be a noticeable spike instantly. A really impressive campaign, a well-placed post or retweet that got the attention of somebody influential. Those could mean massive things for a company. But usually they didn't last long. A big jump in popularity and traffic was great, but what really mattered was sustainability. In order for a company to find and maintain success in the long term, they had to keep up with the traffic and maintain their hold on the attention and interest of customers.

Unfortunately, that wasn't always easy. With a world that had become more and more reliant on technology, people were accustomed to having endless amounts of information and entertainment right at their fingertips. They didn't have the patience to keep up with something that wasn't keeping them fully engaged and offering benefit at all times. Which was why the long-term numbers were more important than any sudden short-term successes. I'd been working on the Freeman Racing campaign long enough to be starting to get those details, and things were looking good.

But that didn't mean letting up. We had to keep pushing, keep giving it our all. I was so invested in what I was working on, I didn't even realize how much time had gone by since getting to work. I didn't know it was already time to take a break for lunch until my brother showed up at the door. We'd both been busier than usual recently with work and even living together, we hadn't been able to sit down and spend as much time together. So, we made the plan to eat lunch together that day. When I looked up and saw him, I glanced down at my phone.

"Is it already time for lunch?" I asked.

"It was time for lunch about an hour ago," he said.

"Oh, I'm sorry," I said. "You should have come and gotten me. I've been so wrapped up in getting these numbers and interacting with the fans, I didn't even realize time was going by. You must be starving. What do you want to eat today?"

"Don't worry about it," Brandon said. "I figured you were probably lost in the land of virtual people, so I got you covered." He held up two large box lunches and a half-gallon of sweet tea. "How does a picnic sound?"

I let out a sigh. "It sounds glorious. Let's go."

I walked out into the hallway and saw he already had the picnic blanket out of the trunk and waiting. Leaning down to pick it up off the floor, I followed him outside and into the heat. As hot as the afternoons were, I would much rather be out in the fresh air than stuck inside any day. We walked right to the field and settled under my favorite tree. Brandon handed me my box, and I eagerly opened it, taking out the egg salad sandwich he'd chosen for me.

"How's that?" he asked, knowing I'd been struggling to eat recently.

"Actually, I feel fine. Maybe we've landed on something."

He grinned and nodded. "That's good to hear. You really should go to the doctor and talk to them about what's been going on. This stomach bug of yours has been going on for a while, and nobody else has gotten sick."

Rather than answering him, I took a giant bite of the egg salad. It was delicious and I suddenly felt like I could eat a dozen of them. Before I was able to take another bite, I heard a strange high-pitched sound followed by a shout. Seconds later, something black and floppy hopped up and snatched my sandwich right out of my hand. Brandon and I laughed as we watched the puppy wrestle with the sandwich for a few seconds before gobbling it down.

Quentin ran up clutching a pink leash. He stopped and hunched over, pressing his hands to his eyes and drawing in a few deep breaths. I wondered how long he'd been running around chasing the puppy.

"Rosie, no," he finally managed to get out.

That made me laugh even harder.

"I think it's too late," I told him.

The black Lab puppy licked her lips and immediately padded over to Brandon. Placing her round paws on his leg, she stretched and strained, sitting and trying to get to his food. But he was holding it over his head so she couldn't get to it. Even as he was holding it away from her, he was laughing and rubbing the puppy with his other hand.

"I'm sorry," Quentin said. "She got away from me."

"No problem," Brandon said. "It just so happens I ordered her an extra sandwich."

The promise of another egg salad sandwich had me digging around in my box, and I promptly pulled it out and unwrapped it. Quentin crouched down and scratched the puppy on the back of her head.

"I just got her yesterday," he told us. "They assured me she would be very easy to train and would do anything I wanted her to do. That's only accurate if what I wanted to do was train myself for a marathon. She hates her leash with a passion, as you have just witnessed. And stealing food is her favorite pastime. As you also just witnessed. I have fed her, I promise."

"It's fine," I reassured him. "We had a chocolate Lab when we were younger. They have a lot of energy, but they're great dogs. And ours ate her fair share of sandwiches, too."

Quentin scooped up the wriggling puppy and gave her a kiss on the side of the face.

"Well, at least that's good to hear. I didn't want to think I had gotten a defective Lab or anything."

I laughed. "She's really precious. Even if she is defective, you should definitely keep her. I didn't know you were even thinking about getting a puppy."

"I wasn't, actually," he told us.

"I've been kind of lonely recently, so getting myself a companion seemed like a good idea."

He was looking directly at me when he said it, and I felt something tremble through me. I didn't know what to do with the surprising revelation, so I didn't respond. Instead, I filed it away for later.

"Did she already have the name Rosie when you got her, or did you name her that?" I asked.

I didn't really know why I asked that question. Whether I actually had any interest in knowing how he came up with a name for his puppy, or if I just wanted him to stay with us a little longer. I wouldn't let myself dwell on the reasoning for very long.

"I gave it to her," he said. "When I went to choose which puppy I wanted, they were all wearing bandanas around their necks. Hers was covered in little roses, and I thought she was such a pretty girl she should have a pretty name."

"What happened to her bandana?" Brandon asked.

"She ate it," Quentin said matter-of-factly.

Brandon and I both laughed. Quentin attached the leash to Rosie's collar, and the puppy immediately started to roll around and thrash like she was being tortured. He lowered down to the grass, and she rolled around, turning her head to try to shoo away the leash.

"Yep," I said. "I can see how much she loves that."

"She's getting used to it," Quentin said. "I'm trying to turn her into one of those dogs I can bring everywhere with me. You know the annoying ones who have their own seat at the Thanksgiving table and ride in the passenger seat of car."

"What's the point of having a dog if they aren't that type of dog?" Brandon asked.

"Exactly," Quentin said with a laugh. He reached down and gently pushed Rosie's face away from her leash. "All right, well, I'm going to go back to attempting to walk her. You two enjoy your lunch. I have a feeling with her around, I'll be having lunch out here a lot more often."

"You're always welcome to join us," Brandon said. "Plenty of tree to go around."

Quentin's eyes moved over to me, and my heart rate picked up a few notches.

"Anytime," I told him.

He smiled and walked away, trying to encourage the puppy to come along with him. She wasn't having it, though, and he ended up dragging her more than she was walking. Soon she even gave that up and relaxed completely, finally starting to roll along the grass as he walked. It didn't seem to bother her at all, and I couldn't help but laugh when Quentin stopped and turned around to give her a look. Rosie looked right back at him, her little tail wagging and beating against the ground. He shook his head and scooped her up, giving her another kiss and cuddling her close to his chest as he walked away.

When he was out of sight, I turned back to my brother. Brandon was watching me, giving me a knowing smile.

"What?" I asked. "Why are you looking at me like that?"

"Really?" he asked. "You're going to give me the innocent act?"

"I don't know what you're talking about," I told him,

taking another bite of my sandwich and reaching into the box for my cheese wafer.

"All right," Brandon said. "If that's how you want to be about it." He finished his sandwich, and we sat in silence for a few moments as he tore a chunk out of his cupcake. "But I think you know what I'm talking about."

I sighed.

"Brandon..."

"Look, I don't know exactly what happened between the two of you but hear me out. I get being hurt. But maybe, just maybe, you two deserve a second chance. I know there are things you aren't telling me about what went down and everything that's going on, but he is still a good guy," he said.

"I know he is," I said.

"Then maybe you should stop being so difficult and believe there could be something for you. There are really good relationships in the world, Merry. And that's coming from a guy who is right smack in the middle of an ugly divorce, so it means extra coming from me."

I swatted him playfully and went back to eating, but his words stuck with me for the rest of the day. He was right. Quentin really was a good guy. But it wasn't so easy as just knowing he was a good guy and being willing to get over the fear of being hurt and try again.

I still had my secret, and that was going to change everything.

35

QUENTIN

Adopting Rosie was somewhat of an impulsive decision. I was going to be the first to admit that. I saw Cole enjoying his puppy so much and brightening up just because of it, and I wanted that. I wanted to have a companion with me and to not feel so lonely and isolated all the time. But I didn't spend a tremendous amount of time thinking about what it was actually going to be like to have that puppy and getting myself ready for it. But I was tossed right into the deep end and thought I was doing fairly well with it considering it was the first time I'd ever actually taken care of a puppy.

My brothers and I had pets when we were growing up, but not a lot of them, and they were never babies. My mother had a soft spot for animals and didn't like the idea of going to a breeder and buying a puppy or kitten, or specifically seeking out a young animal just because it was cute. Instead, she wanted to give a loving home to an animal who needed it, and so we had cats and dogs who are already older when we got them. They were wonderful and I loved having them, but it was definitely a different experience than bringing home a young puppy and starting from scratch. We were both figuring things out together.

One of the first things we figured out was crate training was a big joke. I heard plenty of people rave about it and say it was the only way to go if you were going to have a well-behaved dog. That might be true for some animals and some pet owners, but not so much for Rosie and me. As soon as I picked her up, we went to the pet store together and loaded up on everything I could think of that she might need. Several massive bags of puppy food, dozens of toys, treats, a couple of different collars, a leash, puppy pads, and her crate later, my house felt properly taken over. It was now the home of a puppy and we are going to be very happy together.

That is, until I put her in the crate last night and headed up to bed. I slipped on some covers and turned the light off, and the house echoed with the heartbreaking sound of her wailing downstairs. I went down, added a blanket to her crate, and went back upstairs. The next time I couldn't handle the sound of her crying anymore, I gave her a soft toy to cuddle with. The next time it was a chewy bone to keep her entertained in case she was just too full of energy or I had the one insomniac Lab puppy in existence.

Finally, there was no room left to add anything else into the crate, so I just took her out and brought her upstairs with me. She plopped down onto my bed and immediately burrowed under the blankets at the end. I got in bed, and she curled up cuddled against my feet and was snoring within seconds. That was it. I was done for. I was officially the guy who let his dog sleep in bed with him.

Another thing I had to get used to fairly quickly was waking up to her little pink tongue most of the way up my nose. She licked me awake standing on my chest until I got up and brought her over to her puppy pad, then carried her downstairs for breakfast. I was making a cup of coffee when my phone rang.

"Morning," I said.

"How's Rosie?" Cole asked.

"Is that where we are as friends now?" I asked. "You call to check on my puppy."

"Yes," he said.

"Fair enough. She's doing well. Currently chasing her favorite pink tennis ball around the living room."

"Is she still sleeping in your bed?" He sounded like a concerned grandmother checking to make sure I was raising the new baby in an acceptable way.

"Yes. She has claimed the bottom corner and has her own blanket," I told him.

"Have you even tried the crate again?"

"No," I said. "She cried and wailed. I told you. She hated it. It kept me up and it was heartbreaking. She didn't want to be down on the bottom floor of the house while I was upstairs. She would rather be with me."

"Of course she would rather be with you. But you gotta be consistent. You have to teach her that the crate is her spot and that's where she's comfortable and can go to bed. Just like teaching a baby how to sleep in their crib. It's better for both of you."

"Why?" I asked.

"All those reasons all the experts say it is," Cole said.

"Uh-huh," I said. "That's very compelling evidence. Tell me, Cole, does Bud sleep in a crate?"

"No," he said. "But that's a completely different situation."

"Why?" I asked with a laugh.

"Because I didn't get her a crate," he said.

I laughed again. “Well, that is a very good reason.”

“I’m glad you’re enjoying her. You seem more like yourself again.”

“Me too. Having her around has been great,” I told him.

It really had been. She absolutely did the trick. I didn’t even have the time to be lonely. The wiggly black puppy needed constant attention. I was still battling with her over her leash and learning to walk on it. We were working on learning to sit and lie down, and if I wasn’t trying to teach her something, she wanted me to be patting her, playing with her, feeding her, or running around with her. It was a lot, but she was absolutely worth it.

Rosie was adorable even when she was stealing my food or chewing up my slippers. That was one of the things that surprised me about having her. Everybody always hears about dogs chewing up slippers, but I thought that was just a cliché, something people said because it was a cute, funny thought. I didn’t remember one of our dogs ever chewing up slippers or shoes or anything like that. But Rosie couldn’t get enough of them. She latched right on mine like those slippers were going to get the best of her at any moment. Her little growls were so cute I couldn’t believe she would ever be intimidating to anything.

I loved when she snuggled up under the covers to go to bed or curled up on my feet while I was watching TV. I loved discovering new foods she enjoyed sharing with me and watching her attempt to bury the ones she didn’t like. When it was just the two of us, she was easy to talk to. I didn’t have to be left just with my own thoughts or attempt to untangle things in my brain by myself. She couldn’t answer or give her opinion, but at least I could talk things out. Every now and then she would tilt her head to the side or wag her tail, and I liked to think that was her way of trying it to be a part of the conversation. I never really knew what it meant, but every time she wagged her tail and her tongue slid out in response to Merry's name, I chose to think of it as her giving her endorsement.

I wanted things to work out with Merry more than I ever could have imagined. Almost more than anything I'd ever wanted in the world. She was constantly on my mind, and when I wasn't purposely thinking of her, she would find her way into my thoughts. I could be thinking about something completely different, and suddenly she would show up as a part of it.

Mom called to talk about her idea of renting a huge beach house for all of us to share for a couple of weeks toward the end of summer, and I immediately envisioned Merry stretched out in the sand beside me. I stumbled on an inexplicable marathon of Christmas movies during a late-night weekend movie binge, and instantly I could see Merry and me at my annual Christmas party, cuddling in the lights of the tree and sneaking as many trips under the mistletoe as we could.

I wanted her as part of my life. Not just now, but into the future. I could see us together, building something incredible. But something held me back. I still felt like keeping her at a distance, allowing her to maintain her space as much as she wanted, was still a good plan. It was what I promised her and what she agreed to. I figured if anything changed, she would let me know. That meant I still hung on to my hope. If there was even a hint of a chance that one day she would forgive me, I would hang on to that hope and keep going. It gave me a boost every time I saw her walking around the complex or sitting under her tree having lunch or reading.

That's what I'd come to think of it as. Merry's tree. I

don't know if I'd ever actually noticed that tree before she came to work at the company. Of course, I knew it was there. But I just didn't pay a lot of attention to it. Now I noticed it every time I walked out of the building. My eyes immediately went to it, and I searched the area around its thick trunk to see if she was sitting there. Some days she had files and papers spread out around her and her tablet propped against her thighs. Other times she was sitting on a blanket eating her lunch either with her brother or while reading a book. Sometimes she was just leaned against the tree, her face turned up into the sunlight as she took a few minutes for herself in her busy day.

A week after getting Rosie, she had officially stolen the hearts of everyone at work. The entire crew was completely obsessed with her, and I had to bring her around to let her to see everybody at the start of my day. First thing in the morning, I brought her to each of the offices to visit with everybody, let her spend some time snuggling with Mom while I got my coffee, ate breakfast, or handled some phone calls. Then I reclaimed what she affectionately referred to as her grand-dog and brought her into my office. She had her own bed and an assortment of toys that kept her busy, but her favorite time of day was lunch.

When the middle of the day hit, I took my food and brought her out to run around by the pond. She loved to splash the edge of the water and jump up to try to catch the bugs that fluttered up from the surface. When I was done eating, our tour of visitation brought us to the garages where she was lavished with more attention from the crew. That day, I spent some time with Darren and Dad, then put Rosie on her leash for my daily determined attempt to make her walk like a normal dog.

She was actually doing better, and I could see the light

at the end of the tunnel where she would finally accept her occasional need to wear her leash. We were heading back up to the office, and I glanced over at Merry's tree. She hadn't been there when we first left for lunch, but now she was. She and Brandon were eating box lunches again, and he said something that made her laugh. I wanted to just stop and listen to it for a while. Her laugh was one of the best sounds in the world. She glanced up and noticed me. I waved, and Merry grinned and smiled back.

My heart swelled in my chest. We were making progress. Maybe things would be okay.

36

MERRY

Being pregnant changed everything. That seemed like an incredible understatement and a fairly stupid thing to even comment on considering being pregnant meant I was literally growing another human being inside my body. While it was still difficult sometimes to wrap my head around the idea of there actually being another person developing inside me, a person who would one day be born and go out into the world to affect other people, that was something I'd understood from the very beginning. I knew when I saw the two pink lines on the positive pregnancy test I was going to have a child. At least, the idea was starting to form in my head.

I knew it for certain after I sent Olivia to the store to buy one of every single type of pregnancy test she could find so I could have a panel of results rather than just one. Maybe I was that one person out of however many who got the false positive. That was a thing, right? There were tests that malfunctioned, and it was possible it could tell me I was pregnant when I really wasn't. Or was it false negatives that were the possibility?

It didn't really matter, because while that one test might have been a dud and given me the wrong answer, the other twelve I took throughout the day that day weren't going to be. And they all agreed with the first one. I had a consensus... I was going to be a mother. In that instant, my life changed forever. I knew I was going to have a baby, and one day that baby would grow up. He or she would affect other people in the world. They would make friends. Fall in love. Hurt people. I wasn't too fond of the idea of that last one, but it was an inevitability. I was just going to have to do my best to raise my child well and hope to keep the hurt to a minimum.

My thoughts about my current existence changed. My thoughts about my future changed. My thoughts about my relationships and potential relationships changed.

All that I was ready for. It kind of went without saying those things couldn't stay the same after I found out I was carrying a child. But it was all the other things I wasn't really anticipating. And those might have been hitting me just as hard. After all, it was easier, possibly borderline delusional, but easier, to compartmentalize emotions and not let myself think about anything too far into the future than it was to ignore feeling tired, always having to pee, and discovering new and odd things about my body on a near-daily basis.

Today's discovery was that if I hung upside down for more than ten seconds, I felt like I was going to pass out. It wasn't even an extreme hang. I hadn't strapped myself into huge boots and dangled myself from the closet rod to adjust my spine. I just lay down on my bed, propped my legs up on the wall, and flipped my head back over the edge of the bed. It was something I'd done a million times in my life, a position I assumed when I was really thinking about something.

Not anymore. It took only a matter of seconds before black dots started dancing in front of my eyes and I felt woozy. Olivia saw me press one hand over my eyes and reached out to grab my hand and help me right myself on the mattress.

"You can't hang like that," she told me. "Your body is sending all your blood to the baby to help it grow, so if you do that what's left is going to rush to your head and there won't be any left for anything else."

"Selfish baby," I muttered. I instantly felt guilty and rubbed where my belly would eventually be. "I'm sorry. I didn't mean that, Little Bean. I'm sure you are a very kind and generous baby."

"Little Bean?" Olivia asked. "Are we trying out celebrity-inspired names? Unique and unisex so it works either way?"

"No," I told her. "That's not going to be its name. But I felt like I had to have something to call it. Then I saw it today and it just looked like a little bean to me."

"That's right. Today was your first ultrasound. Did you get pictures?" Olivia asked.

She sounded so excited, and I gestured toward the nightstand where I'd set the strip of black-and-white images. My best friend squealed as she scooped it up and looked at it.

"Do you have any idea what you're looking at?" I asked.

"Of course I do. I've looked at all the ultrasounds for my nieces and nephews," she told me.

"Well, good, because I didn't. The image came up on the screen, and I just stared at it, not having any idea what I was seeing. Do you think that means something?" I asked.

"It means ultrasounds are really blurry and hard to see

anything, especially when you're still as early as you are," she said.

"Or maybe that I'm already destined to be an inadequate mother because I couldn't even distinguish my own embryo from anything else," I commented.

"Don't even start that. The only reason I can tell what's in there is because my siblings have a lot of kids. I learned." I turned my head to stare up at the ceiling again. "All right. Spill. What are you really thinking about?"

"He waved at me," I said.

Olivia let out a groan and toppled backward on the bed. I couldn't really blame her. This was not a new conversation. I spent a good portion of my time now moaning about Quentin to Olivia. And my best friend, bless her, was getting tired of it. She didn't say it, and I knew she never would. She was taking her role as my support system and confidant during this whole thing very seriously, and I knew she wanted to be there for me. But there was only so much she could cover her exasperation when I started talking about him... again.

"Is that it?" she asked.

"It was during lunch. He was walking his puppy up from the garages, and he smiled and waved. It was a genuine smile, like he wanted to come over and talk to me. But he didn't. He just went on by. Brandon was with me, and he's already told me I should maybe give everything with Quentin a second chance. He looked at me like he was waiting for me to get up and chase after him or something."

"And you didn't?" Olivia asked.

There was a slight note of sarcasm in her voice, and I scoffed at her.

"I just sat there watching him. Waiting for him to turn around and come back to sit with me. Can you even believe that? I was sitting there under a tree, holding my sandwich like I was on the front cover of some time-warp family magazine, hoping his puppy would break free from him to come steal it so he'd have to run over."

Finally, Olivia sighed. She reached over and smacked me on the thigh with the back of her hand.

"Just talk to him. That's the only thing that's going to make anything better. You have to talk to him," she said.

"I know."

I let out a long breath, and she opened her eyes a little wider like she was expecting me to say more.

"And?"

"I will. On Monday. I'll go to his office and I'll talk to him and tell him about Little Bean," I told her.

"How?" she asked.

I turned my head to look at her, my eyebrows furrowing together.

"'Quentin, I'm pregnant.' What do you mean how?" I asked.

"Your plan is seriously just walk into the man's office and just blurt out that you're carrying his child? Don't you think you should have more of a lead into that? Somewhat of an approach so you aren't blindsided by what he might say?"

"How am I supposed to prepare for what he might say?" I asked. "I have literally no idea how he's going to react."

"That's why you have to have an approach," Olivia told me. "Cut him off at the pass. Rather than him being the one who gets to react badly, and you haven't responded to it, come up with a way to tell him that covers all your bases first. That way if he's going to have a negative reaction, you've already said everything so he doesn't have to say it to you again."

"All right," I said. "That actually makes sense. I guess I'll tell him it wasn't something I was expecting, but it's happened, and we have to deal with it."

"That's a little bit aggressive," she said.

"You're probably right. What about I tell him about the baby, then say it's both our faults, not just his. I'm not blaming him for anything or saying he did anything wrong. We both willingly slept together, and neither one of us made the decision to stop because we didn't have a condom. So, we're both equally responsible," I suggested.

"I mean, that'll get the job done," Olivia said. "It's not exactly the gentlest or most meaningful of ways to tell a man he's going to be a father. And you left out one important thing."

"What?" I asked.

"How you feel about him," she said.

"I don't need to talk about that right now," I told her. "That's really not the important thing. He needs to know about the baby and not have anything else clouding his thoughts."

"Anything you say," Olivia told me. "As long as he knows about the baby, you can deal with everything else some other time."

She saw right through me. She knew I had a hard time talking about my feelings and would have no idea how to even approach that conversation. But she was right. We could do this one step at a time. First, we talk about Little Bean. We figure out what we're going to do about that, and then we go from there.

"What do you think his family is going to say?" I asked. "I've gotten pretty close to them. Especially Minnie. Do you think she'll get mad about it? Or will the idea of a new grandbaby who isn't covered in fur be enough to ignore the whole mess her son and I made?"

Olivia scooted closer to me across the mattress and rub my hair to comfort me.

"It will be okay," she said soothingly. "It will."

I appreciated her being there for me and doing everything she could to make me feel better. But I wasn't completely convinced. I didn't know if she could really tell me that for sure. This wasn't a situation she had ever been in, and neither of us had any idea how it was going to actually turn out. But for now, I was willing to hold on to it and convince myself she was right. I could pretend it was all going to be okay. As long as it got me through Monday and the conversation I had to have with Quentin, that's all that mattered for now.

37

QUENTIN

Getting Rosie was definitely one of the best decisions I'd ever made, but I was learning she had some unintended consequences. She kept everybody in the complex so happy and reduced stress and anxiety so much, Mom didn't have as much need to bake anymore. Rather than running off to the kitchen and finding solace at the bottom of bags of flour and sugar, she just came to my office and spent some time relishing the never-ending supply of puppy kisses Rosie was more than eager to give her. Then what time she did spend in the kitchen was divided between producing sweets and goodies for us and baking up batch after batch of homemade puppy treats.

I couldn't really blame her. Rosie just got cuter by the day, and they loved her visits. She would lick and cuddle as long as somebody let her or until she toppled over into one of her frequent naps. That was one of my favorite things to watch her do. I loved to see her play and bounce at work, but when she stretched out, her soft little belly up toward the sky, and fell into a deep sleep, it made me feel happy and contented. I liked knowing she was happy with me and

I was giving her a good life. She was doing so much for me, the least I could do was try to give her something in return.

But I was definitely missing my sugar fix. It was probably better for my health, but I didn't really want to think about that. I first got to work in the morning or wandered into the kitchen in the middle of the day looking for something to give me an afternoon boost, I wanted to find a platter of lemon bars or a freshly baked plate of cookies. Instead, I discovered a heavily picked-over tray of apple turnovers and three different types of dog biscuits. She'd even taking the time to use different shapes of cookie cutters for each of the flavors and was standing over one of the plates applying icing.

"Are you putting icing on a cookie for my dog?" I asked.

Mom looked over her shoulder, then turned around and grinned at me.

"Yes, I am," she said. "I found a puppy-friendly recipe that's good for her coat and her little digestive system. And it's delicious, and that's the most important part."

"Did you taste it?" I asked.

She gave me a glare and whipped back around to finish the cookies.

"Yes, I did. It's made completely with human food ingredients, so why shouldn't I? I had to make sure it tasted good for her. Princess Rosie deserves the very best," she said.

I grabbed one of the apple turnovers and balanced it on top of a cup of coffee, scooped up a handful of the other dog biscuits, and headed to my office. Rosie happily trotted along at my heels. She and her leash had come to a begrudging agreement, but I barely even needed to use it anymore. She quickly adapted to just walking along beside me and unless I told her it was okay to run, she stayed close by. I walked into the office and was surprised as hell to see Merry there waiting for me.

"Hi," I said, walking over to my desk and setting down the coffee and turnover. Opening the lid of the cookie jar I'd gotten for Rosie's treats, I dropped the new cookies inside, then fished one back out. Rosie went over to her corner of the office and started examining her bed and each of her toys. She did the same thing every morning. Everything was always in the exact same place where she left it the night before, but the first thing she did when she got into the office was sniff and examine everything as if to confirm it was right.

When she was satisfied, she got onto her bed, circled around a few times, then plopped herself down. I set her cookie down in front of her, and she set her paw on the end of it, making it stand up so she could chew on the other end. That would keep her content for a little while. Now that Rosie was situated, I looked over at Merry.

"Are we done avoiding each other?" I asked.

I meant it as a joke, but it must have fallen flat because Merry flinched. Maybe I was going to need to be more careful with my wording.

"Yes," she said. She hesitated for a second, shifting where she sat on the couch. "Uh. We need to talk."

A joke about the way she said that formed in my mouth. It sounded like she was about to break up with me, but since we'd never actually gone on a date, it wouldn't have been a very effective breakup. Fortunately, this time I thought about what I was going to say before it came out and managed to catch the words on my tongue before they came out of my mouth. That definitely wouldn't have gone over well, especially considering the strained, nervous look I now noticed on her face.

I picked up my coffee and turnover and walked over to sit beside her on the couch. Breaking the turnover in half, I held a piece of it out to her. She took it but didn't bite into it. Instead, she let it sit in her lap as she looked around like she was searching for what she was going to say next. I didn't push. Obviously, there was something on her mind and she was having difficulty finding a way to say it. As much as the stretch of silence was twisting in my stomach and making my heart beat a little faster, I wanted to give her the time to say whatever she needed to stay in the right way. Finally, she let out a sigh and looked at me resolutely.

"I'm not good at doing things like this," she offered, almost like a disclaimer.

"Not good at doing what?" I asked, suddenly feeling dread form in the pit of my stomach. "Are you quitting?"

She laughed, but the sound didn't have any happiness in it.

"I almost wish I was," she said. "At least I've done that before, and it would probably be easier than this. But no. I love working here and don't intend on leaving." She straightened her spine and let out another breath. "What I mean is, I'm not good at talking about my feelings. I have a really hard time with even having them, so acknowledging them and putting them out there for somebody else to know about is a really major challenge to me."

"What do you mean?" I asked.

"Let's just say my history with guys is not great. In fact, among everybody who knew me from when I was younger, I'm known for making bad choices. Really bad choices." She pauses for a second, her eyes widening slightly as she looked off into the distance like she was reliving some of those unfortunate moments of her life. A second later, she shook her head slightly as if coming back into reality. "Anyway, I've done some stupid things. After more than my fair share of bad relationships, I all but gave up on men in general. I figured I would just do this whole life thing on my own.

"It was just easier to think about being alone. As sad as it was and as much as I saw the people around me at finding their partners and getting married and being all joyful and everything, that just wasn't going to happen for me. It wasn't worth the stress and complication. I couldn't trust anybody and didn't want to go through all that over and over again just to get my heart broken. So, I decided I was just going to devote myself to my career and be a confirmed single."

Just sitting there listening to her was so hard. I struggled to keep my hands to myself. All I wanted to do was pull her close to me and hug her. I wanted to comfort her and let her know I was there for her and she could trust me. But I didn't. I continued to listen and stayed still exactly where I was. She needed this. Merry needed the opportunity to express everything that was going on inside her head and know she was being heard. Finally, she finished it and let out a big breath.

"Anyway," she said. "I just want to say I'm sorry for being at least fifty percent at fault for all our problems. It's not totally your fault. I don't want you to think that. I mean, I know you think that. Everybody around you isn't exactly making it easy for you, and I'm sorry about that, too. I am absolutely to blame for the whole mess, too. Because we never talked. And that's what I want to do. I want us to talk now."

I figured she was finished because she looked down at her hands and seemed to notice for the first time that she was holding the half a turnover. Tearing off a corner, she popped it into her mouth, hesitated for a few seconds like she was gauging something about it, then kept eating.

"I'm sorry, too, Merry. I also don't want you to feel like you caused all these problems. I like you. A lot. I don't know if that's come across." It made me smile when she chuckled softly. "But I've been burned by women, too. I can't say I've had many relationships. But the ones I've had have not been good. I've encountered plenty of women who were only after my money and didn't care about me at all. And I never thought that about you, but the possibility of it always makes me a bit jumpy. I came to work on your first day and saw you, and it just threw me for a loop. You were so young and beautiful, and I was instantly drawn to you. But I couldn't help but put up a wall because of what's happened to me. So, I'm sorry, too."

She finished eating and stood. It felt like a punctuation to our conversation. We were good. Both of us had apologized to each other, acknowledged feelings that existed between us, and explained the issues of the past that had kept us apart. It was good progress, but maybe we needed a break now. This was phase one. We'd accomplished it, and in a few days, I could possibly broach the idea of trying to date.

We're walking toward the door when Merry suddenly spun around.

"Fuck it," she muttered, just like I did in her office our first time.

Suddenly her arms were around my neck, her mouth pressed to mine, and I was melting into the kiss.

38

MERRY

Oh, hell.

This was absolutely, one hundred percent not the plan. I went over the plan with myself a dozen times before getting to the office that morning. I stood in my bathroom and looked in the mirror, practicing exactly what I was going to say to him. I'd even practiced on the way to work, saying it in my head over and over so Brandon couldn't hear me. I was completely confident in how I was going to approach it. Just like I told Olivia, this conversation was not going to be about feelings. Feelings were a difficult and sticky subject that I had no interest in getting into with Quentin yet. I wasn't good with feelings. They were hard and made things more complicated, and the very last thing I needed the right then was for things to get more complicated. No, I was just going to go into his office, let him know I was pregnant, and figure out where we were going to go from there.

And somewhere between sitting down on his office sofa to wait for him and eating the piece of apple turnover he inexplicably handed me when he sat down beside me, everything went to hell. The plan flew totally out the window, and before I even realized what was happening, I was knee-deep in talking about emotions and my past. Everything spilled out of me, and I laid it all out for him, vulnerability, trust issues, feelings, and all. Even with all that, I almost made it out of the office. I stood up and started for the door. He was walking with me, ready to send me on my way for the day.

But no. I couldn't let that happen. I had to wrap myself around him again, so there I was kissing him like I couldn't get enough of him. And I never did tell him about Little Bean. But he had his hands on my hips and his tongue in my mouth, and that was just more important at that moment. Not more important than the baby, but definitely more important than me having to share the news right at that second.

I let Quentin pull me to his desk. He took his mouth away from mine only long enough to call out to the puppy chasing a ball around the office.

"Rosie, bad!" he shouted, then dropped his mouth back to mine. He pulled his mouth away again. "Oh, God. I'm going to traumatize her."

It was going to take a lot more than that to stop me.

My hands were clenching, grabbing at anything they could touch. The overwhelming need to feel his skin under the pads of my fingers drove me to slip them through the openings of his shirt, around the buttons. The tantalizing brush against his ab muscles filled me with even more heat in my core and a light-headed sensation rising up my neck and making everything outside of my eyes feel like cotton. Only his lips broke through the haze, and I focused on them, their softness and their fullness, his tongue slipping through them and dancing with mine.

It soothed me and calmed me and focused me on his touch.

We'd backed up to the desk, and now he was working his way around it, guiding me with him with his kiss and fingers working their way down the front of my blouse. One hand slipped inside and cupped my breast around the bra. I wondered if he could feel how much fuller it felt as he gently massaged it. Quickly, he slid back to my center and unclasped the black, lacy cups, and they fell away to the sides, my heavy, plump breasts spilling out into my unbuttoned shirt.

His lips fell from mine and trailed down my neck, his tongue sweeping across my collarbone and into the swell between my breasts. Leaving a thin line of saliva across my chest, he settled on one nipple, taking it into his mouth hungrily and swirling his tongue around it. I leaned my head back and focused on the sensation of my perky nipple hardening in his mouth. His hands slid down my stomach and into the waistband of my skirt, under my panties and to my hot, wet core. I yelped as his powerful fingers touched the sensitive folds of my pussy, and he wasted no time finding my pearl and massaging it firmly, encouraging my clit to open up to him.

I pushed up on my toes until I sat on his desk and pushed away the manila folders and paperweights that would restrict my movements. They clattered on the floor loudly, but I didn't care. Neither did he. He scooted me back, and his hand left my center, reaching for my panties and pulling them down achingly slowly. His eyes widened and his tongue instinctively swept over his lips as he revealed my pussy to the cold air of the air-conditioned room. When he looked back to me, our eyes met, and I kicked away the thin, lacy underwear. They landed on a lamp, and I giggled at the thought of them staying there until the next time he turned on a light.

His hands clasped under my knees and pulled them apart, setting my feet on the top of his desk so I was presented to him. Sitting heavily in his chair, he pulled himself up to me as if I was paperwork he had longed to finish. I closed my eyes and rested back on my hands as his head dipped down into my skirt, and he licked the inside of my thigh. I shuddered in anticipation as he made his way down to my core and swept around my opening, then pulled back to blow a stream of warm air along the line where he licked. I lay back, letting my back rest on papers, and my head fell off the other end of the heavy wooden desk.

A finger traced my opening and slid inside, and I gasped at the feeling of him inside me. I raised my head up to look down my body at him, and we made eye contact as his tongue slid through my folds. I closed my eyes again and lay back again, focusing on the pleasure of his attention to my core. Flicking at my clit with the tip of his tongue, he brought a squeal of delight from me that only seemed to encourage him. His finger plunged into me and began a rhythm of entering and exiting as his tongue swirled over me and brought me to moans that filled the room. I could barely contain myself, and I reached down to fill a hand with his hair as the powerful first orgasm began to rush over my body, filling me with heat and ecstasy and making my legs shake. I clamped my thighs over his ears as my body shook and I climaxed to the beat of his tongue. He lapped me up eagerly and then stood.

I breathed deeply, letting myself come down from the high of the orgasm and enjoy watching him unbuckle his pants. I half expected him to repeat our first desk-based romp and just let his thick cock come through the zipper, but instead, his pants fell away and I could make out the outline of his long engorged dick straining against the boxer briefs he wore. I salivated at the thought of it being inside of me again and sat up. He had just unbuttoned his shirt and tossed it aside when I placed my hand on his chest and gently guided him to sit in his office chair again. Sliding off the desk and letting my shirt and bra fall to the floor, I nestled myself between his legs, sitting on my knees before him.

I grinned as he settled back in his chair, a smile of anticipation and desire stretching across his lips. Sliding my fingers into his waistband, I pulled down on his boxers, and he lifted himself up a little to let it come off him. I relished in watching the reveal of his cock springing out at me, impossibly long and thick and hard. I let the boxers drop away, and he kicked them away as I pushed myself between his legs, letting his cock settle between my breasts. The saliva and sweat made my chest slick, and he nudged forward with his hips at the sensation. I clasped the sides of my breasts and rose and then fell over him, letting him fuck me between my heavy, plump tits. As I reached the bottom, I let my tongue slide out and lick the tip of his head, eliciting a groan from him. When my tongue reached him again, I could taste the salty precum forming and dove down to take him into my mouth.

Letting him slide deeply into my mouth, I let him reach as far back as my throat before sliding back up again, my hand sliding up with it and continuing to stroke him as I raised my lips off him. I glanced at his face to gauge his reaction, but his eyes were shut, his jaw open in a state of pleasure. It fueled me, and I dove back down onto him, tightening my mouth so I was wrapped around his cock and letting him slide in and out of me, my tongue caressing the soft, sensitive areas under it. One hand wrapped firmly around the base and stroked up with every motion, and the other massaged his balls underneath. Moans began to fill the room as he tightened his leg muscles around me, and his hands slid under my hair, at first just moving with me and then guiding me faster. I kept his rhythm and then increased, a hunger for him taking over and making me crave his pleasure, to desire his orgasm as if it were my own.

Two of my own fingers slid down between my thighs, and I touched myself as I stroked him into my mouth. Every sensation was on overload, and I increased my bobbing on him even more, letting him slide as far down my throat as I dared. He moaned loudly and then tightened his fingers in my hair. He held me in place, and I rubbed my clit as he came in my mouth. I suckled him, wanting every drop of his essence, and he shook as he emptied into me. Just as he seemed to be done, I slid my mouth off him, and our eyes met.

"I'm not done," he grumbled.

Lifting me by my chin, his strong, gentle touch guided me to stand. I continued to stroke him until he spun me around and bent me over the desk. I spread my legs to invite him to me, and he wasted no time plunging his thick cock deep inside. He stayed there a moment, and we basked in the glory of his body filling mine. When I had adjusted to him, wrapping around his throbbing mass like a glove, he began to slam into me.

Stars filled my vision as he fucked me deeply, an animalistic grunt welling up from his chest as he took me, dominating me in that moment. I was vulnerable and open and unequivocally his, and he worshiped me with his cock and his hands that clasped at my ass. I could feel the coming rush of another earth-shattering climax, and I clasped onto the desk sides, pushing my hips into him. His speed increased as he pulled me by my hips, and I felt like he stretched me until I could take no more. The wave of the orgasm rolled over me, and a deep, furious growl rolled up from behind as he came again, this time deep inside my pussy, and we throbbed together, riding the wave as one. Sweat rolled down the small of my back as he pressed down into me, emptying himself fully and letting my body milk him. When there was nothing left, he sank down to the floor, pulling me with him, and our mouths crushed into one another for a deep, satisfied kiss.

So, we ended up here again, I thought to myself a few minutes later. Sprawled across each other, sweaty and breathing heavy. Only this time I didn't immediately jump away from him and start to get dressed. We had slid down and were now stretched out on his office floor, my head on his chest and his arm draped lazily over my hip. I lifted my head just enough to look over to where Rosie had moved into the doorway of the bathroom attached to Quentin's office. The puppy was staring at us, her head tilted to the side as if she seemed to be trying to figure out what was happening. I couldn't help but shudder. That wasn't a memory I particularly wanted to hang on to.

"At some point we should try this in a bed," Quentin mumbled, turning to press a kiss to my head.

I could have said anything else, but my stupid after sex brain could only think of one thing.

"I'm pregnant," I said.

There was a beat of silence.

"I mean, I know I'm good. But I don't think you would be able to know that fast," he joked.

"No, Quentin, I'm pregnant."

He sat up, and it forced me to move off him and sit up to face him.

"That's not funny," he said.

I shook my head, starting to say I knew it wasn't, but instead broke down in tears.

39

QUENTIN

Merry's words were ringing through my head, like she was saying them over and over even though I knew she'd only said them once. Well, twice. She had to say them twice because I had to make a stupid joke when she said it the first time. Now I realized that was actually why she came to the office that day. However, we ended up detouring down the path of talking about our feelings, though it was obvious she had come to see me that that day with the intention of telling me the news.

She was pregnant. Merry was pregnant.

That meant I was going to be a father. It was a lot, and we needed to talk about it. But first I needed to make sure she was going to be okay after my stupid comment. Merry looked so terrified, completely falling apart and sobbing as she sat there on my floor. I hated to see her like that, to watch her curl up into herself and hold her knees to her chest as she cried. There were so many thoughts and emotions happening in her, but it was obvious one of them was fear. Not fear because she was pregnant, but fear because she had just told me. She didn't know how I was going to react to what was going to happen, and it was upsetting her to the point it looked like she was about to fall apart.

I got to my feet and dressed as quickly as I could. Not bothering to put my shoes on yet, I collected her clothes and helped her into them. Taking her by her hands, I got her to her feet and led her over to the couch again. We sat down, and I looked over at Rosie. My puppy had been patient and quiet, barely making herself known up until now. It was what I'd asked her to do, and she was being such a good girl, but now I needed her to go back to her bubbly, adorable puppy self.

"Rosie," I called. "Come here, puppy. Come see Merry."

She scrambled over and jumped up on the couch. This was a puppy who didn't need to be asked twice for affection. I patted Merry's lap, and Rosie immediately bounced into it, lifting her little head to lick Merry's face. She circled around a few times, then licked Merry again and again. Merry was still sniffling, but the tears had slowed, and she smiled at the affection from the puppy.

"How long have you known?" I asked.

"A few weeks," she admitted. Her head dropped down for a second before she looked at me again. "I know I should have told you as soon as I found out. You should have been the first call I made, and I should have just been honest with you from the beginning. But I didn't know how. I had no idea how I was supposed to have that conversation with you."

She was obviously struggling to force the words out through the tears that were falling fresh again as she seemed to realize the impact of her holding back the information from me. I reached out and wrapped my arms around her, hugging her tight. It pinned Rosie between us, but she was happy to be able to lick both of us at the same time.

"How did you find out?" I asked.

"You remember when I took a couple of days off?" she asked.

"Yes," I said, reaching up with one hand to brush tears away from her cheeks.

"I was feeling sick. Just tired and queasy, then when I smelled strong food odors or tried to eat much, I got really sick. I thought I just had a stomach bug or a virus of some kind. With everything that had been going on and all the upheaval and change in my life, I honestly wasn't even paying attention. It didn't even occur to me that I'd missed my period. Then I mentioned it to Olivia. She's the one who recognized the symptoms. Her sister and sisters-in-law have been pregnant several times, and she's been there for all of them. She said I sounded just like what her sister felt. So, I asked her to get a test."

"So, she knows?" I asked.

I didn't mean it in a negative way, but she squeezed her eyes closed and looked away again.

"I'm sorry," she said. "I know you should have been the first one to know, but she was there and encouraged me to take the test to see if that's what was happening."

"No," I said. "Don't apologize. I'm glad she could be there for you. That's not something you should have gone through by yourself, and it makes me happy to know you had her."

"She's the only one who knows," she told me. "I haven't told anybody else. Even Brandon. I didn't want anybody else to know until I figure it out how to tell you."

I held her close to me again, kissing the top of her head

and stroking her hair. This wasn't enough. We needed to really talk about this. Not sitting on the couch in my office while the workday went on around us. I wanted to bring her home, to my home. I wanted to tuck her into bed and curl up beside her so we could cuddle and really talk. But first there was something that couldn't wait.

Merry had calmed down enough that I was okay gently moving away from her and getting up to go over to my desk. Rosie happily took my spot, going back to licking and snuggling. I grabbed my phone off my desk and called my mom.

"I need you," I said when she answered the phone.

"Quentin? Is everything all right?" she asked, sounding understandably worried.

"I just need to talk to you. Can you please come to my office?"

"Of course," she said. "I'll be there as fast as I can."

I hung up the phone and turned back to Merry. She was looking at me with widened eyes.

"You called your mother?" she asked.

"Yes," I said. "I can't keep this to myself. I already told you I'm really bad with secrets."

She chuckled, which made me feel better.

"Apparently," she said. "How are you going to do it? She's not the biggest fan of the two of us having anything to do with each other in that way."

"I'll figure it out when she gets here. Don't worry," I said. "This is my mother we're talking about. I've had surprising conversations with her before."

"One like this?" she asked.

"No," I said, sitting back down and wrapping my arms around her again.

That was all I had the opportunity to say. My mother

must have sprouted wings and flown, because she burst into the office door far faster than I would have thought she'd be able to get there. That was good to know.

"What's going on?" she asked, coming into the office and staring at us.

Her eyes locked on where my arms were wrapped around Merry, and I could see her starting to get angry. She'd been clear with me about how she felt regarding the power dynamics of our relationship, and I shouldn't have anything like that to do with one of my employees. I could tell she was about to say something, so I got ahead of her.

"We're getting Rosie a baby," I announced. Beside me, I saw Merry turn to look at me, her eyes even wider. I kept looking at Mom, wanting to make sure she understood what I was saying. "Merry's pregnant."

I waited for the reaction. In that moment, I was very aware it could have gone any direction, but it only took a few seconds for a huge grin to break across her face. My mother was all but glowing as she threw her arms open. Merry and I stood up and let her gather us up into a giant hug. She stepped back from that and then hugged each of us individually.

"I can't believe it," she said. "I'm just so happy. I'm going to be a grandma." Then she looked over at Rosie. "I'm sorry, honey. You will always be my precious grandpuppy."

This seemed to satisfy Rosie, and she jumped over to her bed, dropping down with a sigh as if to say she had done her duty for the day and was going to take a nap. She definitely deserved an extra handful of treats today.

"I know this might be weird or uncomfortable for some people," I said, but Mom immediately shook her head.

"It doesn't matter. It's going to be fine. It'll all work out.

I promise. We will figure it out, and everything will be perfectly fine," she said. "You leave telling your father and your brothers to me. Unless you want to make some sort of announcement."

Merry shook her head. "No. It's fine for you to tell them. Thank you. That actually takes a lot of stress off me."

"Good. You don't need any stress right now. What you need is rest and time together. You two take the rest of the day off," she said.

"Aren't I the one in charge of this company?" I asked.

"Not when I'm on grandma duty. You go home, and we'll all get together tomorrow," she said.

I watched with a lump in my throat as she gathered Merry in her arms again for another hug. She murmured something I couldn't hear into Merry's ear, and Merry smiled, hugging my mother closer. As they pulled apart, Mom looked down at Merry's stomach, searching for any sign of the baby. Merry ran her hand over it.

"There's not much to see yet," she admitted.

"There will be soon enough," Mom said, "and I can't wait to see it."

"Well, before that happens, I'd like to get her home," I said. "We have a lot to talk about."

Wrapping my arm around her shoulders, I guided Merry toward the door.

"Come on, Rosie," she called, and the puppy happily fell into step with us.

I finally got her out to the car and brought her home like I'd wanted to all along. We got to the bedroom, and I gently removed her clothes down to her panties and bra. Stripping down to my boxers, I pulled back the blankets on the bed, and we slipped in. She sighed as she settled down in the crook of my arm. She seemed calm and happy now, and we fell into conversation. It was easy and stress-free. I leaned over and kissed her, just because I wanted to. We had time to figure everything out, and I knew we would. I loved her, and she was finally right where she belonged.

EPILOGUE

QUENTIN - SIX MONTHS LATER

I paced back and forth in the hallway, occasionally smoothing my jacket or reaching up to adjust my tie. This was where I'd been for the last forty-five minutes, and I didn't know exactly what was going on. I turned to the sound of footsteps coming toward me and saw Darren.

"What's going on?" he asked.

"I'm not sure," I said. "The girls scurried off into Merry's office, and I haven't seen them since."

I reached up and wiggled my tie again.

"You all right?" Darren asked.

"This tie is just really uncomfortable. I don't know what's going on with it. It's like it's pushing into something wrong on my neck," I told him.

"Not having second thoughts, are you?" he teased.

"Not even in the slightest," I said. "Well, possibly about the tie. But not about anything else." I adjusted the knot again, but it still wasn't any more comfortable. "How does it look? Does it look right?"

"It looks like you're wearing a suit and tie," Darren said. "You wear them all the time."

"I know, but the difference is when I wear them it's because of work. This is my wedding day. Shouldn't I feel more... like me?" I asked.

Just then, Cole came into the hallway.

"Not to pressure you or anything dude," he said. "Your wedding started twenty-five minutes ago."

"I know," I said. "Not exactly sure what's going on. I haven't heard anything from her in almost an hour."

"I'm not worried about the dress!" Merry's voice suddenly shouted from down the hall. "I just want to be married before I give birth. So, can we please just get on with this?"

I turned to the others with a grin.

"There's my Merry," I said.

Her attitude didn't really surprise me. She was obviously cranky, but she was always cranky at this time of day. Carrying a baby was hard work, and she'd been doing it for eight months now. She was doing a great job of it, right up until around six every evening when she got hungry and angry. Really angry. Which begged the question of why we decided to schedule our wedding for five-thirty.

The door to her office opened down the hall, and Olivia's head popped out.

"Quentin," she called. "Can you come here for a minute?"

"Be right back," I said.

"All right," Cole said. "I guess I'll go back out and tell more jokes to the crowd."

I laughed. He was teasing, of course. At least, I hoped he was. My best friend was many things, but a stand-up comedian was not one of them. Besides, there wasn't really a crowd out there. After I proposed to Merry three months ago, we talked about what we wanted for our wedding. I told her she could have anything, anything that she wanted or envisioned or dreamed of. I wanted her to have the perfect wedding day, even if we waited until well after the baby was born.

She immediately shot down that idea. Not because she didn't want the baby to be at the wedding, but because she didn't want to wait that long for us to get married. We both agreed a small ceremony with just family and close friends sounded ideal. But now it seemed a wrench had been thrown into the plans.

I slipped in through the partially open door to the office and closed it behind me. Merry was standing near the desk, her hands behind her back.

"What's going on?" I asked.

She whipped around and dropped her hands.

"My dress ripped," she said. "I guess I put on a few pounds."

I couldn't help but laugh. Her saying she put on a few pounds was an understatement and she knew it. She joked about it all the time. After taking the first five months of her pregnancy to even begin to show, Merry made up for lost time over the last couple of weeks. Her belly grew round and beautiful, and there was no denying she was very close to delivering our baby boy. Which was good considering her due date was in only three weeks.

"I don't care," I told her. "We could paperclip you into it and hope for the best, and I would still think you are the most beautiful bride I've ever seen."

"That's really sweet of you and I love you more than I could possibly tell you for saying it, but it doesn't take into consideration one important little detail," she said.

"What's that?" I asked.

She took a few steps and the dress opened further, revealing her panties. I laughed harder.

"I can try to fix it," Olivia offered. "I have a sewing kit in my maid-of-honor bag."

"Do you have about a yard and half of extra white satin in there, too?" Merry asked. "Because if not, there's no getting me in this thing. This is a sun's out, buns out situation I don't think anybody in those seats out there is prepared to see today."

"What do you want to do?" I asked.

She gathered up her dress again and turned to me.

"I want to marry you," she said. "I just want to do the ceremony and finally be your wife. I told you when we first talked about the wedding that all the pomp and circumstance doesn't matter to me. All that matters to me is us being married and having our family."

"That's what I want, too," I told her. "So, let's get this done. What else do you have to wear? We'll do this our way."

A few minutes later, I walked back out of the office into the hallway. Cole and Dean both came toward me, concerned looks on their faces. I told them the new plan, and we rushed to get changed. Our wedding started almost an hour late, but I didn't care. Neither did any of the guests. They were all here to see exactly what they were getting: Merry and me walking down the aisle.

For our wedding, the aisle was flower petals sprinkled down the ground to lead toward the pond. We wanted to have our ceremony right there by the water, to commemorate the place where we both knew for the first time we were in love. I stood at the end of the aisle with Cole as our officiant and my brothers by my side. Olivia, Glenda, and a couple of Merry's other friends came down the aisle and took their positions before everybody turned to look at the bride.

She was gorgeous. And I meant it with every fiber of my being. Her arm tucked in the crook of her brother's elbow, holding a bouquet of her favorite sunflowers, she was captivating. Her jean shorts and flowy white top were an upgrade from any bridal gown she could have chosen. We smiled at each other as Brandon escorted her toward me. I shook his hand and thanked him before taking hers and guiding her the rest of the way to stand in front of Cole. There in my jeans and white button-down, with Rosie ready to carry the rings to us hanging from her collar, everything was perfect.

After the ceremony, everyone moved out into the field where we often ate lunch. Several grills and smokers were set up in the grass, and the nearest pavilion had tables laden with salad, corn on the cob, rolls, watermelon, coleslaw, and macaroni and cheese. There were even deviled eggs and cheese wafers from the box lunch shop Merry loved so much.

Away from the cooking meat and the tent set up with a dance floor and music was a small decorated area. Twinkling lights hung in the branches of Merry's favorite tree. A table draped in white fabric and holding a glass vase of sunflowers was set beneath it, ready to accept gifts and cards from the guests. Another table set on the other side of the table had the guest book. When Merry picked it out, she told him she could see us ten years from now sitting down with the guest book on our anniversary and looking through the inscriptions to remember this day.

Everybody dove into the food, loading up plates and sitting down in the nearby pavilion. I saw my parents already in the tent, the only two people on the dance floor.

Merry and I would have our own first dance later. Right now, we all just wanted to relax and enjoy. This wedding was everything I could have wanted. It was a family affair in every sense, and that was perfect. I was so grateful for my parents and the company they'd started so many years ago, the company they'd handed over to me and let me build into what I had today. Including being what brought Merry into my life.

We'd raise our son here. He'd learn about the bikes and how to take care of them. When he got older, maybe we'd train him to race. Then one day, I'd turn the company over to him.

A few hours into the party when the guests were distracted with drinking, dancing, and eating their way through the massive cake, I took Merry's hand and brought her out to the pond. I wanted a few moments just with her. I brought her over to the bench and sat. I kissed her there, in the spot where we conceived our baby, and cuddled her against me, sighing as I listened to Bud and Rosie play and our family celebrate.

THE END

Made in the USA
San Bernardino, CA
11 June 2020

73052066R00161